The Gay Herman Melville Reader

edited by Ken Schellenberg

Gival Press

Arlington, Virginia

Published by Gival Press, an imprint of Gival Press, LLC. For information please write:
Gival Press, LLC, P. O. Box 3812, Arlington, Virginia 22203.

Website: www.givalpress.com

First Edition

ISBN 1-928589-19-7
Library of Congress Control Number 2002108641

Contents

As Always,
For Robert

Introduction

A half-remembered overview of Melville's career according to my college American Lit professor: Melville, who had written very popular sea-faring novels early in his career, saw his reputation collapse after the publication of *Moby Dick*. The novel sold very poorly, and Melville published nothing 'of value' for the rest of his life. He likely would have been forgotten, had not homosexual men circulated copies of *Moby Dick* amongst themselves for decades, creating a cult reputation for the work. The posthumous publication of the novella *Billy Budd* bolstered his popularity among gay men and literary critics, and eventually *Moby Dick* and *Billy Budd* have come to be accepted as 'American Classics.'

More than a decade later, as an out gay man, I was delighted to find my memory validated. I was reading *Closet Writing/Gay Reading: The Case of Melville's Pierre* by James Creech, an essential volume for gay literature buffs. Creech writes that the Melville revival began in earnest after 1920, due in part to interest by gay literati.

The appeal of *Billy Budd* to gay men is clear, of course, Claggart is obviously a closet queen, and the physical appeal of Billy to the other sailors is, for its day, quite explicit. When Benjamin Britten created an opera version (with a plumb part for his lover Peter Pears), he had E.M. Forster write the libretto (Forster, of course, would have his own posthumous gay novel in *Maurice*).

As *Moby Dick*'s reputation and stature grew (it is often called the greatest of American novels), it has acquired that dusty, moldy aura that comes with being an officially sanctioned force-the-kids-to-read-it classic. It's easy to forget just how daring and bold a work it is, and how homoerotically charged. Ishmael and Queequeg spend the night together. Naked, they awake with legs entwined. There's a campy scene of sailors squeezing their hands in whale sperm, but the tone of the writing leads the reader to think that Melville is *really* referring to masturbation.

At least it does to this reader. When I read *Moby Dick*, I read with the awareness of a gay man. There's a charge to certain scenes in Melville that activates my literary gaydar as I "cruise the text" (in that marvelous phrase of Creech's). Melville gives off this charge to this reader in many of his writings. *Mardi*, *Billy Budd*, *Moby Dick*, *Pierre*, *Redburn*, and other of his writings contain passages which connect with me at a visceral level: it's as if the author is winking, saying "I'm one too."

I'll be quick here to fend off some of the charges I'm sure will be lobbed by those who object to the very idea of a "gay" collection of Melville. First, I have absolutely no interest in "proving" whether Melville was actually gay. To me, it is irrelevant to the work itself. Second, I in no way want to convey the impression that *all* of Melville's work was gay or gay-tinged. Entire works (such as *The Confidence Man*) seem to contain no hint of the lavender. Third, I acknowledge that not all readers respond to Melville as I do. Some Claggarty readers may even insist that the notion of Melville making reference to same-gender sex is on its face absurd. All of these scenes, some will say, *could* be interpreted as having no homosexual content.

And yet and yet and yet. Melville's scenes of sailors at sea and on land give off a homoerotic charge that I simply don't find in similar scenes written by, say, Joseph Conrad. As Creech has documented, Melville willingly altered his novels at his publishers' requests to make the same-gender references less obvious. Surely this implies two things: one, that he was quite conscious about referring to same-gender sexuality, and two, that he was willing to let the more obvious references slip away confident in the knowledge that other less obvious references remained. And I'm confident that other gay readers will resond in the same way, and perhaps even straight readers. I was with a straight friend at a bookstore recently, and we started talking about *Moby Dick*. He too was struck by homoerotic passages in the text (and interestingly enough, the very passages he regards as gay are the ones I had chosen to include in this volume).

With our 20/20 gaydar tuned and targeted at his other works, it's fairly easy to see that Melville addresses same-gender attraction throughout his career, a remarkable thing when you consider that the word "homosexual" was not even invented until his career was half-over. In this collection, we'll start with the scenes from *Moby Dick* that were mentioned above, and then move to selections from his lesser-known novels.

White-Jacket is an early Melville novel. The excerpt we've included here describes how sailors pass their time on board a ship.

Redburn follows the adventures of a young American sailor. In the excerpt, the young inexperienced Redburn picks up an attractive young British man who turns out to be a bit of a drama queen. They go to London, to what appears to be a male brothel.

In the second excerpt from *Redburn,* we'll follow the pair onto the boat where they enjoy the flute playing (!) of another sailor. This is another example of Melville in his camp mode: *double entendres* comes out in full force in this excerpt.

Pierre, written immediately after *Moby Dick,* continues to this day to be one of the least known novels by a major American novelist. It was viciously attacked at the time of its publication, and few have ventured to read it since. While few have actually read it, opinions of it are not hard to come by. Even Elizabeth Hardwick, dismissing *Pierre* in her fine short biography of Melville, admits she hasn't actually read the book. This is quite a pity, because *Pierre* is an extremely bold attack on bourgeois values. It features scenes of masturbation (Pierre jerks off to pictures of his father) and incest (Pierre and his sister). To me, it reads like a John Waters film: daringly camp. To some literary critics, Melville was working out his unrequited love for Nathaniel Hawthorne. To others, it's a rant against the American Reading Public (and the publishing industry) for rejecting *Moby Dick.* In any case, it's a fascinating novel.

The last selection in the book is, like *Moby Dick,* familiar. We have included the entire text of *Billy Budd,* one of the key homoerotic texts in American literature.

Regrettably, I've passed over *Mardi, Typee,* and *Omoo.* While these novels are not without interest for the gay reader, they simply don't lend themselves to abridgement.

I'll end these introductory notes with a request of you, gentle reader. Should I have overlooked a particular lavender passage of Melville that you think ought to have been included, please don't hesitate to contact me. I would certainly love to know what I've overlooked. I can be reached via e-mail at *gaylit@givalpress.com.*

You'd Better Get Used To That Sort Of Thing

This excerpt from Moby Dick *takes place early in the novel. Ismael, the narrator, is still on land and is still a "virgin" as a sailor. Making his way to the sea, he stays overnight at the Spouter Inn. At the inn, he is told he must share a bed with the magnificently tattooed Queequeg. He has second thoughts, but in the end they sleep together "in a most loving manner." The homoerotic implications of this excerpt are so obvious as not to require further explanation.*

This excerpt contains chapters 3 and 4 of the novel. The title is contained within Melville's text, but is not his title for either chapter.

Entering that gable-ended Spouter-Inn, you found yourself in a wide, low, straggling entry with old-fashioned wainscots, reminding one of the bulwarks of some condemned old craft. On one side hung a very large oil-painting so thoroughly besmoked, and every way defaced, that in the unequal cross-lights by which you viewed it, it was only by diligent study and a series of systematic visits to it, and careful inquiry of the neighbors, that you could any way arrive at an understanding of its purpose. Such unaccountable masses of shades and shadows, that at first you almost thought some ambitious young artist, in the time of the New England hags, had endeavored to delineate chaos bewitched. But by dint of much and earnest contemplation, and oft repeated ponderings, and especially by throwing open the little window towards the back of the entry, you at last come to the conclusion that such an idea, however wild, might not be altogether unwarranted.

But what most puzzled and confounded you was a long, limber, portentous, black mass of something hovering in the centre of the picture over three blue, dim, perpendicular lines floating in a nameless yeast. A boggy, soggy, squitchy picture truly, enough to drive a nervous man distracted. Yet was there a sort of indefinite, half-attained, unimaginable sublimity about it that fairly froze you to it, till you involuntarily took an oath with yourself to find out what that marvellous painting meant. Ever and anon a bright, but, alas, deceptive idea would dart you through.—It's the Black Sea in a midnight gale.—It's the unnatural combat of the four primal elements.—It's a blasted heath.—It's a Hyperborean winter scene.—It's the breaking-up of the icebound stream of Time. But at last all these fancies yielded to that one portentous something in the picture's midst. *That* once found out, and all the rest were plain. But stop; does it not bear a faint resemblance to a gigantic fish? even the great leviathan himself?

In fact, the artist's design seemed this: a final theory of my own, partly based upon the aggregated opinions of many aged persons with whom I conversed upon the subject. The picture represents a Cape-Horner in a great hurricane; the half-foundered ship weltering there with its three dismantled masts alone visible; and an exasperated whale, purposing to spring clean over the craft, is in the enormous act of impaling himself upon the three mast-heads.

The opposite wall of this entry was hung all over with a heathenish array of monstrous clubs and spears. Some were thickly set with glittering teeth resembling ivory saws; others were tufted with knots of human hair; and one was sickle-shaped, with a vast handle, sweeping round like the segment made in the new-mown grass by a long-armed mower. You shuddered as you gazed, and wondered what monstrous cannibal and savage could ever have gone a death-harvesting with such a hacking, horrifying implement. Mixed with these were rusty old whaling lances and harpoons all broken and deformed. Some were storied weapons. With this once long lance, now wildly elbowed, fifty years ago did Nathan Swain kill fifteen whales between a sunrise and a sunset. And that harpoon—so like a corkscrew now—was flung in Javan seas, and run away with by a whale, years afterwards slain off the Cape of Blanco. The original iron entered nigh the tail, and, like a restless needle sojourning in the body of a man, travelled full forty feet, and at last was found imbedded in the hump.

Crossing this dusky entry, and on through yon low-arched way—cut through what in old times must have been a great central chimney with fireplaces all round—you enter the public room. A still duskier place is this, with such low ponderous beams above, and such old wrinkled planks beneath, that you would almost fancy you trod some old craft's cockpits, especially of such a howling night, when this corner-anchored old ark rocked so furiously. On one side stood a long, low, shelf-like table covered with cracked glass cases, filled with dusty rarities gathered from this wide world's remotest nooks. Projecting from the further angle of the room stands a dark-looking den—the bar—a rude attempt at a right whale's head. Be that how it may, there stands the vast arched bone of the whale's jaw, so wide, a coach might almost drive beneath it. Within are shabby shelves, ranged round with old decanters, bottles, flasks; and in those jaws of swift destruction, like another cursed Jonah (by which name indeed they called him), bustles a little withered old man, who, for their money, dearly sells the sailors deliriums and death.

Abominable are the tumblers into which he pours his poison. Though true cylinders without—within, the villanous green goggling glasses deceitfully tapered downwards to a cheating bottom. Parallel meridians rudely pecked into the glass, surround these footpads' goblets. Fill to *this* mark, and your charge is but a penny; to *this* a penny more; and so on to the full glass—the Cape Horn measure, which you may gulp down for a shilling.

Upon entering the place I found a number of young seamen gathered about a table, examining by a dim light divers specimens of *skrimshander*. I sought the landlord, and telling him I desired to be accommodated with a room, received for answer that his house was full—not a bed unoccupied. "But avast," he added, tapping his forehead, "you haint no objections to sharing a harpooneer's blanket, have ye? I s'pose you are goin' a whalin', so you'd better get used to that sort of thing."

I told him that I never liked to sleep two in a bed; that if I should ever do so, it would depend upon who the harpooneer might be, and that if he (the landlord) really had no other place for me, and the harpooneer was not decidedly objectionable, why rather than wander further about a strange town on so bitter a night, I would put up with the half of any decent man's blanket.

"I thought so. All right; take a seat. Supper?—you want supper? Supper'll be ready directly."

I sat down on an old wooden settle, carved all over like a bench on the Battery. At one end a ruminating tar was still further adorning it with his jack-knife, stooping over and diligently working away at the space between his legs. He was trying his hand at a ship under full sail, but he didn't make much headway, I thought.

At last some four or five of us were summoned to our meal in an adjoining room. It was cold as Iceland—no fire at all—the landlord said he couldn't afford it. Nothing but two dismal tallow candles, each in a winding sheet. We were fain to button up our monkey jackets, and hold to our lips cups of scalding tea with our half frozen fingers. But the fare was of the most substantial kind—not only meat and potatoes, but dumplings; good heavens! dumplings for supper! One young fellow in a green box coat, addressed himself to these dumplings in a most direful manner.

"My boy," said the landlord, "you'll have the nightmare to a dead sartainty."

"Landlord," I whispered, "that aint the harpooneer is it?"

"Oh, no," said he, looking a sort of diabolically funny, "the harpooneer is a dark complexioned chap. He never eats dumplings, he don't—he eats nothing but steaks, and he likes 'em rare."

"The devil he does," says I. "Where is that harpooneer? Is he here?"

"He'll be here afore long," was the answer.

I could not help it, but I began to feel suspicious of this "dark complexioned" harpooneer. At any rate, I made up my mind that if it so turned out that we should sleep together, he must undress and get into bed before I did.

Supper over, the company went back to the bar-room, when, knowing not what else to do with myself, I resolved to spend the rest of the evening as a looker on.

Presently a rioting noise was heard without. Starting up, the landlord cried, "That's the Grampus's crew. I seed her reported in the offing this morning; a three years' voyage, and a full ship. Hurrah, boys; now we'll have the latest news from the Feegees."

A tramping of sea boots was heard in the entry; the door was flung open, and in rolled a wild set of mariners enough. Enveloped in their shaggy watch coats, and with their heads muffled in woollen comforters, all bedarned and ragged, and their beards stiff with icicles, they seemed an eruption of bears from Labrador. They had just landed from their boat, and this was the first house they entered. No wonder, then, that they made a straight wake for the whale's mouth—the bar—when the wrinkled little old Jonah, there officiating, soon poured them out brimmers all round. One complained of a bad cold in his head, upon which Jonah mixed him a pitch-like potion of gin and molasses, which he swore was a sovereign cure for all colds and catarrhs whatsoever, never mind of how long standing, or whether caught off the coast of Labrador, or on the weather side of an ice-island.

The liquor soon mounted into their heads, as it generally does even with the arrantest topers newly landed from sea, and they began capering about most obstreperously.

I observed, however, that one of them held somewhat aloof, and though he seemed desirous not to spoil the hilarity of his shipmates by his own sober face, yet upon the whole he refrained from making as much noise as the rest. This man interested me at once; and since the sea-gods had ordained that he should soon become my shipmate (though but a sleeping-partner one, so far as this narrative is concerned), I will here venture upon a little description of him. He stood full six feet in height, with noble shoulders, and a chest like a coffer-dam. I have seldom seen such brawn in a man. His face was deeply brown and burnt, making his white teeth dazzling by the contrast; while in the deep shadows of his eyes floated some reminiscences that did not seem to give him much joy. His voice at once announced that he was a Southerner, and from his fine stature, I thought he must be one of those tall mountaineers from the Alleghanian Ridge in Virginia. When the revelry of his companions had mounted to its height, this man slipped away unobserved, and I saw no more of him till he became my comrade on the sea. In a few minutes, however, he was missed by his shipmates, and being, it seems, for some reason a huge favorite with them, they raised a cry of "Bulkington! Bulkington! where's Bulkington?" and darted out of the house in pursuit of him.

It was now about nine o'clock, and the room seeming almost supernaturally quiet after these orgies, I began to congratulate myself upon a little plan that had occurred to me just previous to the entrance of the seamen.

No man prefers to sleep two in a bed. In fact, you would a good deal rather not sleep with your own brother. I don't know how it is, but people like to be private when they are sleeping. And when it comes to sleeping with an unknown stranger, in a strange inn, in a strange town, and that stranger a harpooneer, then your objections indefinitely multiply. Nor was there any earthly reason why I as a sailor should sleep two in a bed, more than anybody else; for sailors no more sleep two in a bed at sea, than bachelor Kings do ashore. To be sure they all sleep together in one apartment, but you have your own hammock, and cover yourself with your own blanket, and sleep in your own skin.

The more I pondered over this harpooneer, the more I abominated the thought of sleeping with him. It was fair to presume that being a harpooneer, his linen or woolen, as the case might be, would not be of the tidiest, certainly none of the finest. I began to twitch all over. Besides, it was getting late, and my decent harpooneer ought to be home and going bedwards. Suppose now, he should tumble in upon me at midnight—how could I tell from what vile hole he had been coming?

"Landlord! I've changed my mind about that harpooneer.—I shan't sleep with him. I'll try the bench here."

"Just as you please; I'm sorry I cant spare ye a tablecloth for a mattress, and it's a plaguy rough board here"—feeling of the knots and notches.

"But wait a bit, Skrimshander; I've got a carpenter's plane there in the bar—wait, I say, and I'll make ye snug enough." So saying he procured the plane; and with his old silk handkerchief first dusting the bench, vigorously set to planing away at my bed, the while grinning like an ape. The shavings flew right and left; till at last the plane-iron came bump against an indestructible knot. The landlord was near spraining his wrist, and I told him for heaven's sake to quit—the bed was soft enough to suit me, and I did not know how all the planing in the world could make eider down of a pine plank. So gathering up the shavings with another grin, and throwing them into the great stove in the middle of the room, he went about his business, and left me in a brown study.

I now took the measure of the bench, and found that it was a foot too short; but that could be mended with a chair. But it was a foot too narrow, and the other bench in the room was about four inches higher than the planed one—so there was no yoking them. I then placed the first bench lengthwise along the only clear space against the wall, leaving a little interval between, for my back to settle down in. But I soon found that there came such a draught of cold air over me from under the sill of the window, that this plan would never do at all, especially as another current from the rickety door met the one from the window, and both together formed a series of small whirlwinds in the immediate vicinity of the spot where I had thought to spend the night.

The devil fetch that harpooneer, thought I, but stop, couldn't I steal a march on him—bolt his door inside, and jump into his bed, not to be wakened by the most violent knockings? It seemed no bad idea but upon second thoughts I dismissed it. For who could tell but what the next morning, so soon as I popped out of the room, the harpooneer might be standing in the entry, all ready to knock me down!

Still, looking round me again, and seeing no possible chance of spending a sufferable night unless in some other person's bed, I began to think that after all I might be cherishing unwarrantable prejudices against this unknown harpooneer. Thinks I, I'll wait awhile; he must be dropping in before long. I'll have a good look at him then, and perhaps we may become jolly good bedfellows after all—there's no telling.

But though the other boarders kept coming in by ones, twos, and threes, and going to bed, yet no sign of my harpooneer.

"Landlord!" said I, "what sort of a chap is he—does he always keep such late hours?" It was now hard upon twelve o'clock.

The landlord chuckled again with his lean chuckle, and seemed to be mightily tickled at something beyond my comprehension. "No," he answered, "generally he's an airley bird—airley to bed and airley to rise—yea, he's the bird what catches the worm.—But to-night he went out a peddling, you see, and I don't see what on airth keeps him so late, unless, may be, he can't sell his head."

"Can't sell his head?—What sort of a bamboozingly story is this you are telling me?" getting into a towering rage. "Do you pretend to say, landlord, that this harpooneer is actually engaged this blessed Saturday night, or rather Sunday morning, in peddling his head around this town?"

"That's precisely it," said the landlord, "and I told him he couldn't sell it here, the market's overstocked."

"With what?" shouted I.

"With heads to be sure; ain't there too many heads in the world?"

"I tell you what it is, landlord," said I, quite calmly, "you'd better stop spinning that yarn to me—I'm not green."

"May be not," taking out a stick and whittling a toothpick, "but I rayther guess you'll be done *brown* if that ere harpooneer hears you a slanderin' his head."

"I'll break it for him," said I, now flying into a passion again at this unaccountable farrago of the landlord's.

"It's broke a'ready," said he.

"Broke," said I—"*broke*, do you mean?"

"Sartain, and that's the very reason he can't sell it, I guess."

"Landlord," said I, going up to him as cool as Mt. Hecla in a snow-storm—"landlord, stop whittling. You and I must understand one another, and that too without delay. I come to your house and want a bed; you tell me you can only give me half a one; that the other half belongs to a certain harpooneer. And about this harpooneer, whom I have not yet seen, you persist in telling me the most mystifying and exasperating stories, tending to beget in me an uncomfortable feeling towards the man whom you design for my bedfellow—a sort of connexion, landlord, which is an intimate and confidential one in the highest degree. I now demand of you to speak out and tell me who and what this harpooneer is, and whether I shall be in all respects safe to spend the night with him. And in the first place, you will be so good as to unsay that story about selling his head, which if true I take to be good evidence that this harpooneer is stark mad, and I've no idea of sleeping with a madman; and you, sir, *you* I mean, landlord, *you*, sir, by trying

19

to induce me to do so knowingly would thereby render yourself liable to a criminal prosecution."

"Wall," said the landlord, fetching a long breath, "that's a purty long sarmon for a chap that rips a little now and then. But be easy, be easy, this here harpooneer I have been tellin' you of has just arrived from the south seas, where he bought up a lot of 'balmed New Zealand heads (great curios, you know), and he's sold all on 'em but one, and that one he's trying to sell to-night, cause to-morrow's Sunday, and it would not do to be sellin' human heads about the streets when folks is goin' to churches. He wanted to, last Sunday, but I stopped him just as he was goin' out of the door with four heads strung on a string, for all the airth like a string of onions."

This account cleared up the otherwise unaccountable mystery, and showed that the landlord, after all, had had no idea of fooling me—but at the same time what could I think of a harpooneer who stayed out of a Saturday night clean into the holy Sabbath, engaged in such a cannibal business as selling the heads of dead idolators?

"Depend upon it, landlord, that harpooneer is a dangerous man."

"He pays reg'lar," was the rejoinder. "But come, it's getting dreadful late, you had better be turning flukes—it's a nice bed: Sal and me slept in that ere bed the night we were spliced. There's plenty of room for two to kick about in that bed; it's an almighty big bed that. Why, afore we give it up, Sal used to put our Sam and little Johnny in the foot of it. But I got a dreaming and sprawling about one night, and somehow, Sam got pitched on the floor, and came near breaking his arm. Arter that, Sal said it wouldn't do. Come along here, I'll give ye a glim in a jiffy;" and so saying he lighted a candle and held it towards me, offering to lead the way. But I stood irresolute; when looking at a clock in the corner, he exclaimed "I vum it's Sunday—you won't see that harpooneer to-night; he's come to anchor somewhere—come along then; *do* come; *won't* ye come?"

I considered the matter a moment, and then up stairs we went, and I was ushered into a small room, cold as a clam, and furnished, sure enough, with a prodigious bed, almost big enough indeed for any four harpooneers to sleep abreast.

"There," said the landlord, placing the candle on a crazy old sea chest that did double duty as a wash-stand and centre table; "there, make yourself comfortable now; and good night to ye." I turned round from eyeing the bed, but he had disappeared.

Folding back the counterpane, I stooped over the bed. Though none of the most elegant, it yet stood the scrutiny tolerably well. I then glanced round the room; and besides the bedstead and centre table, could see no other furniture belonging to the place, but a rude shelf, the four walls, and a papered fireboard representing a man striking a whale. Of things not properly belonging to the room, there was a hammock lashed up, and thrown upon the floor in one corner; also a large seaman's bag, containing the harpooneer's wardrobe, no doubt in lieu of a land trunk. Likewise, there was a parcel of outlandish bone fish hooks on the shelf over the fire-place, and a tall harpoon standing at the head of the bed.

But what is this on the chest? I took it up, and held it close to the light, and felt it, and smelt it, and tried every way possible to arrive at some satisfactory conclusion concerning it. I can compare it to nothing but a large door mat, ornamented at the edges with little tinkling tags something like the stained porcupine quills round an Indian moccasin. There was a hole or slit in the middle of this mat, the same as in South American ponchos. But could it be possible that any sober harpooneer would get into a door mat, and parade the streets of any Christian town in that sort of guise? I put it on, to try it, and it weighed me down like a hamper, being uncommonly shaggy and thick, and I thought a little damp, as though this mysterious harpooneer had been wearing it of a rainy day. I went up in it to a bit of glass stuck against the wall, and I never saw such a sight in my life. I tore myself out of it in such a hurry that I gave myself a kink in the neck.

I sat down on the side of the bed, and commenced thinking about this head-peddling harpooneer, and his door mat. After thinking some time on the bed-side, I got up and took off my monkey jacket, and then stood in the middle of the room thinking. I then took off my coat, and thought a little more in my shirt sleeves. But beginning to feel very cold now, half undressed as I was, and remembering what the landlord said about the harpooneer's not coming home at all that night, it being so very late, I made no more ado, but jumped out of my pantaloons and boots, and then blowing out the light tumbled into bed, and commended myself to the care of heaven.

Whether that mattress was stuffed with corn-cobs or broken crockery, there is no telling, but I rolled about a good deal, and could not sleep for a long time. At last I slid off into a light doze, and had pretty nearly made a good offing towards the land of Nod, when I heard a heavy footfall in the passage, and saw a glimmer of light come into the room from under the door.

Lord save me, thinks I, that must be the harpooneer, the infernal head-peddler. But I lay perfectly still, and resolved not to say a word till spoken to. Holding a light in one hand, and that identical New Zealand head in the other, the stranger entered the room, and without looking towards the bed, placed his candle a good way off from me on the floor in one corner, and then began working away at the knotted cords of the large bag I before spoke of as being in the room. I was all eagerness to see his face, but he kept it averted for some time while employed in unlacing the bag's mouth. This accomplished, however, he turned round—when, good heavens! what a sight! Such a face! It was of a dark, purplish, yellow color, here and there stuck over with large, blackish looking squares. Yes, it's just as I thought, he's a terrible bedfellow; he's been in a fight, got dreadfully cut, and here he is, just from the surgeon. But at that moment he chanced to turn his face so towards the light, that I plainly saw they could not be sticking-plasters at all, those black squares on his cheeks. They were stains of some sort or other. At first I knew not what to make of this; but soon an inkling of the truth occurred to me. I remembered a story of a white man—a whaleman too—who, falling among the cannibals, had been tattooed by them. I concluded that this harpooneer, in the course of his distant voyages, must have met with a similar adventure. And what is it, thought I, after all! It's only his outside; a man can be honest in any sort of skin. But then, what to make of his unearthly complexion, that part of it, I mean, lying round about, and completely independent of the squares of tattooing. To be sure, it might be nothing but a good coat of tropical tanning; but I never heard of a hot sun's tanning a white man into a purplish yellow one. However, I had never been in the South Seas; and perhaps the sun there produced these extraordinary effects upon the skin. Now, while all these ideas were passing through me like lightning, this harpooneer never noticed me at all. But, after some difficulty having opened his bag, he commenced fumbling in it, and presently pulled out a sort of tomahawk, and a seal-skin wallet with the hair on. Placing these on the old chest in the middle of a room, he then took the New Zealand head—a ghastly thing enough—and crammed it down into the bag. He now took off his hat—a new beaver hat—when I came nigh singing out with fresh surprise. There was no hair on his head—none to speak of at least—nothing but a small scalp-knot twisted up on his forehead. His bald purplish head now looked for all the world like a mildewed skull. Had not the stranger stood between me and the door, I would have bolted out of it quicker than ever I bolted a dinner.

Even as it was, I thought something of slipping out of the window, but it was the second floor back. I am no coward, but what to make of this head-peddling purple rascal altogether passed my comprehension. Ignorance is the parent of fear, and being completely nonplussed and confounded about the stranger, I confess I was now as much afraid of him as if it was the devil himself who had thus broken into my room at the dead of night. In fact, I was so afraid of him that I was not game enough just then to address him, and demand a satisfactory answer concerning what seemed inexplicable in him.

Meanwhile, he continued the business of undressing, and at last showed his chest and arms. As I live, these covered parts of him were checkered with the same squares as his face; his back, too, was all over the same dark squares; he seemed to have been in a Thirty Years' War, and just escaped from it with a sticking-plaster shirt. Still more, his very legs were marked, as if a parcel of dark green frogs were running up the trunks of young palms. It was now quite plain that he must be some abominable savage or other shipped aboard of a whaleman in the South Seas, and so landed in this Christian country. I quaked to think of it. A peddler of heads too—perhaps the heads of his own brothers. He might take a fancy to mine—heavens! look at that tomahawk!

But there was no time for shuddering, for now the savage went about something that completely fascinated my attention, and convinced me that he must indeed be a heathen. Going to his heavy grego, or wrapall, or dreadnaught, which he had previously hung on a chair, he fumbled in the pockets, and produced at length a curious little deformed image with a hunch on its back, and exactly the color of a three days' old Congo baby. Remembering the embalmed head, at first I almost thought that this black manikin was a real baby preserved some similar manner. But seeing that it was not at all limber, and that it glistened a good deal like polished ebony, I concluded that it must be nothing but a wooden idol, which indeed it proved to be. For now the savage goes up to the empty fire-place, and removing the papered fire-board, sets up this little hunch-backed image, like a tenpin, between the andirons. The chimney jambs and all the bricks inside were very sooty, so that I thought this fire-place made a very appropriate little shrine or chapel for his Congo idol.

I now screwed my eyes hard towards the half hidden image, feeling but ill at ease meantime—to see what was next to follow. First he takes about a double handful of shavings out of his grego pocket, and places them carefully before the idol; then laying a bit of ship biscuit on top and applying the flame from the lamp, he kindled the shavings into a sacrificial blaze. Presently, after many hasty snatches into the fire, and still hastier withdrawals of his fingers (whereby he seemed to be scorching them badly), he at last succeeded in drawing out the biscuit; then blowing off the heat and ashes a little, he made a polite offer of it to the little negro. But the little devil did not seem to fancy such dry sort of fare at all; he never moved his lips. All these strange antics were accompanied by still stranger guttural noises from the devotee, who seemed to be praying in a sing-song or else singing some pagan psalmody or other, during which his face twitched about in the most unnatural manner. At last extinguishing the fire, he took the idol up very unceremoniously, and bagged it again in his grego pocket as carelessly as if he were a sportsman bagging a dead woodcock.

All these queer proceedings increased my uncomfortableness, and see-ing him now exhibiting strong symptoms of concluding his business op-erations, and jumping into bed with me, I thought it was high time, now or never, before the light was put out, to break the spell in which I had so long been bound.

But the interval I spent in deliberating what to say, was a fatal one. Taking up his tomahawk from the table, he examined the head of it for an instant, and then holding it to the light, with his mouth at the handle, he puffed out great clouds of tobacco smoke. The next moment the light was extinguished, and this wild cannibal, tomahawk between his teeth, sprang into bed with me. I sang out, I could not help it now; and giving a sudden grunt of astonishment he began feeling me.

Stammering out something, I knew not what, I rolled away from him against the wall, and then conjured him, whoever or whatever he might be, to keep quiet, and let me get up and light the lamp again. But his guttural responses satisfied me at once that he but ill comprehended my meaning.

"Who-e debel you?"—he at last said—"you no speak-e, dam-me, I kill-e." And so saying the lighted tomahawk began flourishing about me in the dark.

"Landlord, for God's sake, Peter Coffin!" shouted I. "Landlord! Watch! Coffin! Angels! save me!"

"Speak-e! tell-ee me who-ee be, or dam-me, I kill-e!" again growled the cannibal, while his horrid flourishings of the tomahawk scattered the hot tobacco ashes about me till I thought my linen would get on fire. But thank heaven, at that moment the landlord came into the room light in

24

hand, and leaping from the bed I ran up to him.

"Don't be afraid now," said he, grinning again, "Queequeg here wouldn't harm a hair of your head."

"Stop your grinning," shouted I, "and why didn't you tell me that that infernal harpooneer was a cannibal?"

"I thought ye know'd it;—didn't I tell ye, he was a peddlin' heads around town?—but turn flukes again and go to sleep. Queequeg, look here—you sabbee me, I sabbee you—this man sleepe you—you sabbee?"—

"Me sabbee plenty"—grunted Queequeg, puffing away at his pipe and sitting up in bed.

"You gettee in," he added, motioning to me with his tomahawk, and throwing the clothes to one side. He really did this in not only a civil but a really kind and charitable way. I stood looking at him a moment. For all his tattooings he was on the whole a clean, comely looking cannibal. What's all this fuss I have been making about, thought I to myself—the man's a human being just as I am: he has just as much reason to fear me, as I have to be afraid of him. Better sleep with a sober cannibal than a drunken Christian.

"Landlord," said I, "tell him to stash his tomahawk there, or pipe, or whatever you call it; tell him to stop smoking, in short, and I will turn in with him. But I don't fancy having a man smoking in bed with me. It's dangerous. Besides, I ain't insured."

This being told to Queequeg, he at once complied, and again politely motioned me to get into bed—rolling over to one side as much as to say—I won't touch a leg of ye.

"Good night, landlord," said I, "you may go."

I turned in, and never slept better in my life.

Upon waking next morning about daylight, I found Queequeg's arm thrown over me in the most loving and affectionate manner. You had almost thought I had been his wife. The counterpane was of patchwork, full of odd little parti-colored squares and triangles; and this arm of his tattooed all over with an interminable Cretan labyrinth of a figure, no two parts of which were of one precise shade—owing I suppose to his keeping his arm at sea unmethodically in sun and shade, his shirt sleeves irregularly rolled up at various times—this same arm of his, I say, looked for all the world like a strip of that same patchwork quilt. Indeed, partly lying on it as the arm did when I first awoke, I could hardly tell it from the quilt, they so blended their hues together; and it was only by the sense of weight and pressure that I could tell that Queequeg was hugging me.

My sensations were strange. Let me try to explain them. When I was a child, I well remember a somewhat similar circumstance that befell me; whether it was a reality or a dream, I never could entirely settle. The circumstance was this. I had been cutting up some caper or other—I think it was trying to crawl up the chimney, as I had seen a little sweep do a few days previous; and my stepmother who, somehow or other, was all the time whipping me, or sending me to bed supperless,—my mother dragged me by the legs out of the chimney and packed me off to bed, though it was only two o'clock in the afternoon of the 21st June, the longest day in year in our hemisphere. I felt dreadfully. But there was no help for it, so up stairs I went to my little room in the third floor, undressed myself as slowly as possible so as to kill time, and with a bitter sigh got between the sheets.

I lay there dismally calculating that sixteen entire hours must elapse before I could hope for a resurrection. Sixteen hours in bed! the small of my back ached to think of it. And it was so light too; the sun shining in at the window, and a great rattling of coaches in the streets, and the sound of gay voices all over the house. I felt worse and worse—at last I got up, dressed, and softly going down in my stockinged feet, sought out my stepmother, and suddenly threw myself at her feet, beseeching her as a particular favor to give me a good slippering for my misbehaviour: anything indeed but condemning me to lie abed such an unendurable length of time. But she was the best and most conscientious of stepmothers, and back I had to go to my room. For several hours I lay there broad awake, feeling a great deal worse than I have ever done since, even from the greatest subsequent misfortunes. At last I must have fallen into a troubled nightmare of a doze; and slowly waking from it—half steeped in dreams—I opened my eyes, and the before sunlit room was now wrapped in outer darkness. Instantly I felt a shock running through all my frame; nothing was to be seen, and nothing was to be heard; but a supernatural hand seemed placed in mine. My arm hung over the counterpane, and the nameless, unimaginable, silent form or phantom, to which the hand belonged, seemed closely seated by my bed-side. For what seemed ages piled on ages, I lay there, frozen with the most awful fears, not daring to drag away my hand; yet ever thinking that if I could but stir it one single inch, the horrid spell would be broken. I knew not how this consciousness at last glided away from me; but waking in the morning, I shudderingly remembered it all, and for days and weeks and months afterwards I lost myself in confounding attempts to explain the mystery. Nay, to this very hour, I often puzzle myself with it.

Now, take away the awful fear, and my sensations at feeling the supernatural hand in mine were very similar, in the strangeness, to those which I experienced on waking up and seeing Queequeg's pagan arm thrown round me. But at length all the past night's events soberly recurred, one by one, in fixed reality, and then I lay only alive to the comical predicament. For though I tried to move his arm—unlock his bridegroom clasp—yet, sleeping as he was, he still hugged me tightly, as though naught but death should part us twain. I now strove to rouse him—"Queequeg!"—but his only answer was a snore. I then rolled over, my neck feeling as if it were in a horse-collar; and suddenly felt a slight scratch. Throwing aside the counterpane, there lay the tomahawk sleeping by the savage's side, as if it were a hatchet-faced baby. A pretty pickle, truly, thought I; abed here in a strange house in the broad day, with a cannibal and a tomahawk! "Queequeg!—in the name of goodness, Queequeg, wake!" At length, by dint of much wriggling, and loud and incessant expostulations upon the unbecomingness of his hugging a fellow male in that matrimonial sort of style, I succeeded in extracting a grunt; and presently, he drew back his arm, shook himself all over like a Newfoundland dog just from the water, and sat up in bed, stiff as a pike-staff, looking at me, and rubbing his eyes as if he did not altogether remember how I came to be there, though a dim consciousness of knowing something about me seemed slowly dawning over him. Meanwhile, I lay quietly eyeing him, having no serious misgivings now, and bent upon narrowly observing so curious a creature. When, at last, his mind seemed made up touching the character of his bedfellow, and he became, as it were, reconciled to the fact; he jumped out upon the floor, and by certain signs and sounds gave me to understand that, if it pleased me, he would dress first and then leave me to dress afterwards, leaving the whole apartment to myself. Thinks I, Queequeg, under the circumstances, this is a very civilized overture; but, the truth is, these savages have an innate sense of delicacy, say what you will; it is marvellous how essentially polite they are. I pay this particular compliment to Queequeg, because he treated me with so much civility and consideration, while I was guilty of great rudeness; staring at him from the bed, and watching all his toilette motions; for the time my curiosity getting the better of my breeding. Nevertheless, a man like Queequeg you don't see every day, he and his ways were well worth unusual regarding.

He commenced dressing at top by donning his beaver hat, a very tall one, by the by, and then—still minus his trowsers—he hunted up his boots. What under the heavens he did it for, I cannot tell, but his next movement was to crush himself—boots in hand, and hat on—under the bed; when, from sundry violent gaspings and strainings, I inferred he was hard at work booting himself; though by no law of propriety that I ever heard of, is any man required to be private when putting on his boots. But Queequeg, do you see, was a creature in the transition stage—neither caterpillar nor butterfly. He was just enough civilized to show off his outlandishness in the strangest possible manners. His education was not yet completed. He was an undergraduate. If he had not been a small degree civilized, he very probably would not have troubled himself with boots at all; but then, if he had not been still a savage, he never would have dreamt of getting under the bed to put them on. At last, he emerged with his hat very much dented and crushed down over his eyes, and began creaking and limping about the room, as if, not being much accustomed to boots, his pair of damp, wrinkled cowhide ones—probably not made to order either—rather pinched and tormented him at the first go off of a bitter cold morning.

Seeing, now, that there were no curtains to the window, and that the street being very narrow, the house opposite commanded a plain view into the room, and observing more and more the indecorous figure that Queequeg made, staving about with little else but his hat and boots on; I begged him as well as I could, to accelerate his toilet somewhat, and particularly to get into his pantaloons as soon as possible. He complied, and then proceeded to wash himself. At that time in the morning any Christian would have washed his face; but Queequeg, to my amazement, contented himself with restricting his ablutions to his chest, arms, and hands. He then donned his waistcoat, and taking up a piece of hard soap on the wash-stand centre table, dipped it into water and commenced lathering his face. I was watching to see where he kept his razor, when lo and behold, he takes the harpoon from the bed corner, slips out the long wooden stock, unsheathes the head, whets it a little on his boot, and striding up to the bit of mirror against the wall, begins a vigorous scraping, or rather harpooning of his cheeks. Thinks I, Queequeg, this is using Rogers's best cutlery with a vengeance. Afterwards I wondered the less at this operation when I came to know of what fine steel the head of a harpoon is made, and how exceedingly sharp the long straight edges are always kept.

The rest of his toilet was soon achieved, and he proudly marched out of the room, wrapped up in his great pilot monkey jacket, and sporting his harpoon like a marshal's baton.

A Squeeze Of The Hand

This excerpt from Moby Dick *details the process of squeezing whale sperm. Melville writes here in a manner that would, a century later, be called "camp". He's ostensibly discussing extracting the valuable sperm from a whale, but sentences such as "let us all squeeze ourselves into each other; let us squeeze ourselves universally into the very milk and sperm of kindness" seem to indicate that he's thinking of another type of sperm extraction. In these "over the top" passages, Melville seems to revel in an extended dirty joke.*

This excerpt contains the first half of chapter 94 of the novel. The title is Melville's own.

That whale of Stubb's, so dearly purchased, was duly brought to the Pequod's side, where all those cutting and hoisting operations previously detailed, were regularly gone through, even to the baling of the Heidelberg Tun, or Case.

While some were occupied with this latter duty, others were employed in dragging away the larger tubs, so soon as filled with the sperm; and when the proper time arrived, this same sperm was carefully manipulated ere going to the try-works, of which anon.

It had cooled and crystallized to such a degree, that when, with several others, I sat down before a large Constantine's bath of it, I found it strangely concreted into lumps, here and there rolling about in the liquid part. It was our business to squeeze these lumps back into fluid. A sweet and unctuous duty! No wonder that in old times sperm was such a favorite cosmetic. Such a clearer! such a sweetener! such a softener! such a delicious mollifier! After having my hands in it for only a few minutes, my fingers felt like eels, and began, as it were, to serpentine and spiralize.

As I sat there at my ease, cross-legged on the deck; after the bitter exertion at the windlass; under a blue tranquil sky; the ship under indolent sail, and gliding so serenely along; as I bathed my hands among those soft, gentle globules of infiltrated tissues, wove almost within the hour; as they richly broke to my fingers, and discharged all their opulence, like fully ripe grapes their wine; as I snuffed up that uncontaminated aroma,—literally and truly, like the smell of spring violets; I declare to you, that for the time I lived as in a musky meadow; I forgot all about our horrible oath; in that inexpressible sperm, I washed my hands and my heart of it; I almost began to credit the old Paracelsan superstition that sperm is of rare virtue in allaying the heat of anger: while bathing in that bath, I felt divinely free from all ill-will, or petulance, or malice, of any sort whatsoever.

Squeeze! squeeze! squeeze! all the morning long; I squeezed that sperm till I myself almost melted into it; I squeezed that sperm till a strange sort of insanity came over me; and I found myself unwittingly squeezing my co-laborers' hands in it, mistaking their hands for the gentle globules. Such an abounding, affectionate, friendly, loving feeling did this avocation beget; that at last I was continually squeezing their hands, and looking up into their eyes sentimentally; as much as to say,—Oh! my dear fellow beings, why should we longer cherish any social acerbities, or know the slightest ill-humor or envy! Come; let us squeeze hands all round; nay, let us all squeeze ourselves into each other; let us squeeze ourselves universally into the very milk and sperm of kindness.

Would that I could keep squeezing that sperm for ever! For now, since by many prolonged, repeated experiences, I have perceived that in all cases man must eventually lower, or at least shift, his conceit of attainable felicity; not placing it anywhere in the intellect or the fancy; but in the wife, the heart, the bed, the table, the saddle, the fire-side; the country; now that I have perceived all this, I am ready to squeeze case eternally. In thoughts of the visions of the night, I saw long rows of angels in paradise, each with his hands in a jar of spermaceti.

A Mysterious Night In London

These excerpts from the novel Redburn *are quite remarkable. Redburn, a young American sailor, picks up a young man (Harry Bolton) while on shore leave in Liverpool. Great friends, they make a trip to London to a male whorehouse, where Bolton has what is evidently an assignation. Redburn (a bit of a drama queen) becomes quite agitated while waiting for Bolton to finish his business. Is this perhaps an early example of self-hatred due to Redburn's inability to accept his sexuality? Certainly, it's a theme we'll see later in the Claggart character in* Billy Budd.

These excerpts reprint selections from chapters 44 through 46. There are two breaks in the text: several paragraphs from chapters 44 and 45 have been removed.

The title of this excerpt is Melville's own title for chapter 46.

It was the day following my Sunday stroll into the country, and when I had been in England four weeks or more, that I made the acquaintance of a handsome, accomplished, but unfortunate youth, young Harry Bolton. He was one of those small, but perfectly formed beings, with curling hair, and silken muscles, who seem to have been born in cocoons. His complexion was a mantling brunette, feminine as a girl's; his feet were small; his hands were white; and his eyes were large, black, and womanly; and, poetry aside, his voice was as the sound of a harp.

But where, among the tarry docks, and smoky sailor-lanes and by-ways of a seaport, did I, a battered Yankee boy, encounter this courtly youth?

Several evenings I had noticed him in our street of board inn-houses, standing in the doorways, and silently regarding the animated scenes without. His beauty, dress, and manner struck me as so out of place in such a street, that I could not possibly divine what had transplanted this delicate exotic from the conservatories of some Regent-street to the untidy potato-patches of Liverpool.

At last I suddenly encountered him at the sign of the Baltimore Clipper. He was speaking to one of my shipmates concerning America; and from something that dropped, I was led to imagine that he contemplated a voyage to my country. Charmed with his appearance, and all eagerness to enjoy the society of this incontrovertible son of a gentleman — a kind of pleasure so long debarred me — I smoothed down the skirts of my jacket, and at once accosted him; declaring who I was, and that nothing would afford me greater delight than to be of the least service, in imparting any information concerning America that he needed.

He glanced from my face to my jacket, and from my jacket to my face, and at length, with a pleased but somewhat puzzled expression, begged me to accompany him on a walk.

We rambled about St George's Pier until nearly midnight; but before we parted, with uncommon frankness, he told me many strange things respecting his history.

According to his own account, Harry Bolton was a native of Bury St Edmunds, a borough in Suffolk, not very far from London, where he was early left an orphan, under the charge of an only aunt. Between his aunt and himself, his mother had divided her fortune; and young Harry thus fell heir to a portion of about five thousand pounds.

Being of a roving mind, as he approached his majority he grew restless of the retirement of a country place; especially as he had no profession or business of any kind to engage his attention.

In vain did Bury, with all its fine old monastic attractions, lure him to abide on the beautiful banks of her Larke, and under the shadow of her stately and storied old Saxon tower.

By all my rare old historic associations, breathed Bury; by my Abbey-gate, that bears to this day the arms of Edward the Confessor; by my carved roof of the old church of St Mary's, which escaped the low rage of the bigoted Puritans; by the royal ashes of Mary Tudor, that sleep in my midst; by my Norman ruins, and by all the old abbots of Bury, do not, oh Harry! abandon me. Where will you find shadier walks than under my lime-trees? where lovelier gardens than those within the old walls of my monastery, approached through my lordly Gate? Or if, oh Harry! indifferent to my historic mosses, and caring not for my annual verdure, thou must needs be lured by other tassels, and wouldst fain, like the Prodigal, squander thy patrimony, then, go not away from old Bury to do it. For here, on Angel-Hill, are my coffee and card-rooms, and billiard saloons, where you may lounge away your mornings, and empty your glass and your purse as you list.

In vain. Bury was no place for the adventurous Harry, who must needs hie to London, where in one winter, in the company of gambling sportsmen and dandies, he lost his last sovereign.

What now was to be done? His friends made interest for him in the requisite quarters, and Harry was soon embarked for Bombay, as a midshipman in the East India service; in which office he was known as a '*guinea-pig*', a humorous appellation then bestowed upon the middies of the Company. And considering the perversity of his behavior, his delicate form, and soft complexion, and that gold guineas had been his bane, this appellation was not altogether, in poor Harry's case, inapplicable.

He made one voyage, and returned; another, and returned; and then threw up his warrant in disgust. A few weeks' dissipation in London, and again his purse was almost drained; when, like many prodigals, scorning to return home to his aunt, and amend — though she had often written him the kindest of letters to that effect — Harry resolved to precipitate himself upon the New World, and there carve out a fresh fortune.

With this object in view, he packed his trunks, and took the first train for Liverpool. Arrived in that town, he at once betook himself to the docks, to examine the American shipping, when a new crotchet entered his brain, born of his old sea reminiscences. It was to assume duck trowsers and tarpaulin, and gallantly cross the Atlantic as a sailor. There was a dash of romance in it; a taking abandonment; and a scorn of fine coats, which exactly harmonized with his reckless contempt, at the time, for all past conventionalities.

Thus determined, he exchanged his trunk for a mahogany chest; sold some of his superfluities; and moved his quarters to the sign of the Gold Anchor in Union-street.

After making his acquaintance, and learning his intentions, I was all anxiety that Harry should accompany me home in the Highlander, a desire to which he warmly responded.

Nor was I without strong hopes that he would succeed in an application to the captain; inasmuch as during our stay in the docks, three of our crew had left us, and their places would remain unsupplied till just upon the eve of our departure.

And here, it may as well be related, that owing to the heavy charges to which the American ships long staying in Liverpool are subjected, from the obligation to continue the wages of their seamen, when they have little or no work to employ them, and from the necessity of boarding them ashore, like lords, at their leisure, captains interested in the ownership of their vessels, are not at all indisposed to let their sailors abscond, if they please, and thus forfeit their money; for they well know that, when wanted, a new crew is easily to be procured, through the crimps of the port.

Though he spake English with fluency, and from his long service in the vessels of New York, was almost an American to behold, yet Captain Riga was in fact a Russian by birth, though this was a fact that he strove to conceal. And though extravagant in his personal expenses, and even indulging in luxurious habits, costly as Oriental dissipation, yet Captain Riga was a niggard to others; as, indeed, was evinced in the magnificent stipend of three dollars, with which he requited my own valuable services. Therefore, as it was agreed between Harry and me, that he should offer to ship as a '*boy*', at the same rate of compensation with myself, I made no doubt that, incited by the cheapness of the bargain, Captain Riga would gladly close with him; and thus, instead of paying sixteen dollars a month to a thorough-going tar, who would consume all his rations, buy up my young blade of Bury, at the rate of half a dollar a week; with the cheering prospect, that by the end of the voyage, his fastidious palate would be the means of leaving a handsome balance of salt beef and pork in the *harness-cask*.

With part of the money obtained by the sale of a few of his velvet vests, Harry, by my advice, now rigged himself in a Guernsey frock and man-of-war trowsers; and thus equipped, he made his appearance, one fine morning, on the quarter-deck of the Highlander, gallantly doffing his virgin tarpaulin before the redoubtable Riga.

No sooner were his wishes made known, than I perceived in the captain's face that same bland, benevolent, and bewitchingly merry expression, that had so charmed, but deceived me, when, with Mr Jones, I had first accosted him in the cabin.

Alas, Harry! thought I, — as I stood upon the forecastle looking astern where they stood, — that '*gallant, gay deceiver*' shall not altogether cajole you, if Wellingborough can help it. Rather than that should be the case, indeed, I would forfeit the pleasure of your society across the Atlantic. At this interesting interview the captain expressed a sympathetic concern touching the sad necessities, which he took upon himself to presume must have driven Harry to sea; he confessed to a warm interest in his future welfare; and did not hesitate to declare that, in going to America, under such circumstances, to seek his fortune, he was acting a manly and spirited part; and that the voyage thither, as a sailor, would be an invigorating preparative to the landing upon a shore, where he must battle out his fortune with Fate.

He engaged him at once; but was sorry to say, that he could not provide him a home on board till the day previous to the sailing of the ship;

and during the interval, he could not honor any drafts upon the strength of his wages.

However, glad enough to conclude the agreement upon any terms at all, my young blade of Bury expressed his satisfaction; and full of admiration at so urbane and gentlemanly a sea-captain, he came forward to receive my congratulations.

'Harry,' said I, 'be not deceived by the fascinating Riga — that gay Lothario of all inexperienced, sea-going youths, from the capital or the country; he has a Janus-face, Harry; and you will not know him when he gets you out of sight of land, and mounts his cast-off coats and trowsers. For *then* he is another personage altogether, and adjusts his character to the shabbiness of his integuments. No more condolings and sympathy then; no more blarney; he will hold you a little better than his boots, and would no more think of addressing you than of invoking wooden Donald, the figure-head on our bows.'

And I further admonished my friend concerning our crew, particularly of the diabolical Jackson, and warned him to be cautious and wary. I told him, that unless he was somewhat accustomed to the rigging, and could furl a royal in a squall, he would be sure to subject himself to a sort of treatment from the sailors, in the last degree ignominious to any mortal who had ever crossed his legs under mahogany.

And I played the inquisitor, in cross-questioning Harry respecting the precise degree in which he was a practical sailor; — whether he had a giddy head; whether his arms could bear the weight of his body; whether, with but one hand on a shroud, a hundred feet aloft in a tempest, he felt he could look right to windward and beard it.

To all this, and much more, Harry rejoined with the most off-hand and confident air; saying that in his '*guinea-pig*' days, he had often climbed the masts and handled the sails in a gentlemanly and amateur way; so he made no doubt that he would very soon prove an expert tumbler in the Highlander's rigging.

His levity of manner, and sanguine assurance, coupled with the constant sight of his most unseamanlike person — more suited to the Queen's drawing-room than a ship's forecastle — bred many misgivings in my mind. But after all, every one in this world has his own fate intrusted to himself; and though we may warn, and forewarn, and give sage advice, and indulge in many apprehensions touching our friends; yet our friends, for the most part, will '*gang their ain gate*'; and the most we can do is, to hope for the best.

Still, I suggested to Harry, whether he had not best cross the sea as a steerage passenger, since he could procure enough money for that; but no, he was bent upon going as a sailor.

I now had a comrade in my afternoon strolls, and Sunday excursions; and as Harry was a generous fellow, he shared with me his purse and his heart. He sold off several more of his fine vests and trowsers, his silver-keyed flute and enameled guitar; and a portion of the money thus furnished was pleasantly spent in refreshing ourselves at the road-side inns in the vicinity of the town.

Reclining side by side in some agreeable nook, we exchanged our experiences of the past. Harry enlarged upon the fascinations of a London life; described the curricle he used to drive in Hyde Park; gave me the measurement of Madame Vestris' ankle; alluded to his first introduction at a club to the madcap Marquis of Waterford; told over the sums he had lost upon the turf on a Derby day; and made various but enigmatical allusions to a certain Lady Georgiana Theresa, the noble daughter of an anonymous earl.

Even in conversation, Harry was a prodigal; squandering his aristocratic narrations with a careless hand; and, perhaps, sometimes spending funds of reminiscences not his own.

As for me, I had only my poor old uncle the senator to fall back upon; and I used him upon all emergencies, like the knight in the game of chess; making him hop about, and stand stifly up to the encounter, against all my fine comrade's array of dukes, lords, curricles, and countesses.

In these long talks of ours, I frequently expressed the earnest desire I cherished, to make a visit to London; and related how strongly tempted I had been one Sunday, to walk the whole way, without a penny in my pocket. To this, Harry rejoined, that nothing would delight him more, than to show me the capital; and he even meaningly but mysteriously hinted at the possibility of his doing so, before many days had passed. But this seemed so idle a thought, that I only imputed it to my friend's good-natured, rattling disposition, which sometimes prompted him to out with any thing, that he thought would be agreeable. Besides, would this fine blade of Bury be seen, by his aristocratic acquaintances, walking down Oxford-street, say, arm ~in arm with the sleeve of my shooting-jacket? The thing was preposterous; and I began to think, that Harry, after all, was a little bit disposed to impose upon my Yankee credulity.

Luckily, my Bury blade had no acquaintance in Liverpool, where, indeed, he was as much in a foreign land, as if he were already on the shores of Lake Erie; so that he strolled about with me in perfect abandonment; reckless of the cut of my shooting-jacket; and not caring one whit who might stare at so singular a couple.

But once, crossing a square, faced on one side by a fashionable hotel, he made a rapid turn with me round a corner; and never stopped, till the square was a good block in our rear. The cause of this sudden retreat, was a remarkably elegant coat and pantaloons, standing upright on the hotel steps, and containing a young buck, tapping his teeth with an ivory-headed riding-whip.

'Who was he, Harry?' said I.

'My old chum, Lord Lovely,' said Harry, with a careless air, 'and Heaven only knows what brings Lovely from London.'

'A lord?' said I, starting; 'then I must look at him again', for lords are very scarce in Liverpool.

Unmindful of my companion's remonstrances, I ran back to the corner; and slowly promenaded past the upright coat and pantaloons on the steps.

It was not much of a lord to behold; very thin and limber about the legs, with small feet like a doll's, and a small, glossy head like a seal's. I had seen just such looking lords standing in sentimental attitudes in front of Palmo's in Broadway.

However, he and I being mutual friends of Harry's, I thought something of accosting him, and taking counsel concerning what was best to be done for the young prodigal's welfare; but upon second thoughts I thought best not to intrude; especially, as just then my lord Lovely stepped to the open window of a hashing carriage which drew up; and throwing himself into an interesting posture, with the sole of one boot vertically exposed, so as to show the stamp on it — a coronet — fell into a sparkling conversation with a magnificent white satin hat, surmounted by a regal marabout feather, inside.

I doubted not, this lady was nothing short of a peeress; and thought it would be one of the pleasantest and most charming things in the world, just to seat myself beside her, and otder · the coachman to take us a drive into the country.

But, as upon further consideration, I imagined that the peeress might decline the honor of my company, since I had no formal card of introduction; I marched on, and rejoined my companion, whom I at once endeavored to draw out, touching Lord Lovely; but he only made mysterious an-swers; and turned off the conversation, by allusions to his visits to Ickworth in Suffolk, the magnificent seat of the Most Noble Marquis of Bristol, who had repeatedly assured Harry that he might consider Ickworth his home.

Now, all these accounts of marquises and Ickworths, and Harry's hav-ing been hand in glove with so many lords and ladies, began to breed some suspicions concerning the rigid morality of my friend, as a teller of the truth. But, after all, thought I to myself, who can prove that Harry has fibbed?

Certainly, his manners are polished, he has a mighty easy address; and there is nothing altogether impossible about his having consorted with the master of Ickworth, and the daughter of the anonymous earl. And what right has a poor Yankee, like me, to insinuate the slightest suspicion against what he says? What little money he has, he spends freely; he can not be a polite blackleg, for I am no pigeon to pluck; so that is out of the question; — perish such a thought, concerning my own bosom friend!

But though I drowned all my suspicions as well as I could, and ever cherished toward Harry a heart, loving and true; yet, spite of all this, I never could entirely digest some of his imperial reminiscences of high life. I was very sorry for this; as at times it made me feel ill at ease in his com-pany; and made me hold back my whole soul from him; when, in its loneli-ness, it was yearning to throw itself into the unbounded bosom of some immaculate friend.

It might have been a week after our glimpse of Lord Lovely, that Harry, who had been expecting a letter, which, he told me, might possibly alter his plans; one afternoon came bounding on board the ship, and sprang down the hatchway into the *between-decks*, where, in perfect solitude, I was engaged picking oakum; at which business the mate had set me, for want of any thing better.

'Hey for London, Wellingborough!' he cried. 'Off tomorrow! first train — be there the same night — come! I have money to rig you all out — drop that hangman's stuff there, and away! Pah! how it smells here! Come; up you jump!'

I trembled with amazement and delight.

London? it could not be! — and Harry — how kind of him I he was then indeed what he seemed. But instantly I thought of all the circum-stances of the case, and was eager to know what it was that had induced this sudden departure.

In reply my friend told me, that he had received a remittance, and had hopes of recovering a considerable sum, lost in some way that he chose to conceal.

'But how am I to leave the ship, Harry?' said I; 'they will not let me go, will they? You had better leave me behind, after all; I don't care very much about going; and besides, I have no money to share the expenses.'

This I said, only pretending indifference, for my heart was jumping all the time.

'Tut! my Yankee bantam,' said Harry; 'look here!' and he showed me a handful of gold.

'But they are yours, and not mine, Harry,' said I.

'Yours and mine, my sweet fellow,' exclaimed Harry. 'Come, sink the ship, and let's go!'

'But you don't consider, if I quit the ship, they'll be sending a constable after me, won't they?'

'What! and do you think, then, they value your services so highly? Ha! ha! — Up, up, Wellingborough: I can't wait.'

True enough. I well knew that Captain Riga would not trouble himself much, if I *did* take French leave of him. So, without further thought of the matter, I told Harry to wait a few moments, till the ship's bell struck four; at which time I used to go to supper, and be free for the rest of the day.

* * * *

'No time to lose,' said Harry, 'come along.'

He called a cab: in an under tone mentioned the number of a house in some street to the driver; we jumped in, and were off.

As we rattled over the boisterous pavements, past splendid squares, churches, and shops, our cabman turning corners like a skater on the ice, and all the roar of London in my ears, and no end to the walls of brick and mortar; I thought New York a hamlet, and Liverpool a coal-hole, and myself somebody else: so unreal seemed every thing about me. My head was spinning round like a top, and my eyes ached with much gazing; particularly about the corners, owing to my darting them so rapidly, first this side, and then that, so as not to miss any thing; though, in truth, I missed much.

'Stop,' cried Harry, after a long while, putting his head out of the window, all at once — 'stop! do you hear, you deaf man? you have passed the house — No. 40 I told you — that's it — the high steps there, with the purple light!'

The cabman being paid, Harry adjusting his whiskers and mustache, and bidding me assume a lounging look, pushed his hat a little to one side, and then locking arms, we sauntered into the house; myself feeling not a little abashed; it was so long since I had been in any courtly society. It was some semi-public place of opulent entertainment; and far surpassed any thing of the kind I had ever seen before.

The floor was tesselated with snow-white, and russet-hued marbles; and echoed to the tread, as if all the Paris catacombs were underneath. I started with misgivings at that hollow, boding sound, which seemed sighing with a subterraneous despair, through ah the magnificent spectacle around me; mocking it, where most it glared.

The walls were painted so as to deceive the eye with interminable colonnades; and groups of columns of the finest Scagliola work of variegated marbles — emerald-green and gold, St Pons veined with silver, Sienna with porphyry — supported a resplendent fresco ceiling, arched like a bower, and thickly clustering with mimic grapes. Through all the East of this foliage, you spied in a crimson dawn, Guido's ever youthful Apollo, driving forth the horses of the sun. From sculptured stalactites of vine-boughs, here and there pendent hung galaxies of gas lights, whose vivid glare was softened by pale, cream-colored, porcelain spheres, shedding over the place a serene, silver flood; as if every porcelain sphere were a moon; and this superb apartment was the moon-lit garden of Portia at Belmont; and the gentle lovers, Lorenzo and Jessica, lurked somewhere among the vines.

At numerous Moorish looking tables, supported by Caryatides of turbaned slaves, sat knots of gentlemanly men, with cut decanters and taper-waisted glasses, journals and cigars, before them.

To and fro ran obsequious waiters, with spotless napkins thrown over their arms, and making a profound salaam, and hemming deferentially, whenever they uttered a word.

At the further end of this brilliant apartment, was a rich mahogony turret-like structure, partly built into the wall, and communicating with rooms in the rear. Behind, was a very handsome florid old man, with snow-white hair and whiskers, and in a snow-white jacket — he looked like an almond tree in blossom — who seemed to be standing, a polite sentry over the scene before him; and it was he, who mostly ordered about the waiters; and with a silent salute, received the silver of the guests.

Our entrance excited little or no notice; for every body present seemed exceedingly animated about concerns of their own; and a large group was gathered around one tall, military looking gentleman, who was reading some India war-news from the Times, and commenting on it, in a very loud voice, condemning, in tote, the entire campaign.

We seated ourselves apart from this group, and Harry, rapping on the table, called for wine; mentioning some curious foreign name.

The decanter, filled with a pale yellow wine, being placed before us, and my comrade having drunk a few glasses; he whispered me to remain where I was, while he withdrew for a moment.

I saw him advance to the turret-like place, and exchange a confidential word with the almond tree there, who immediately looked very much surprised, — I thought, a little disconcerted, — and then disappeared with him.

While my friend was gone, I occupied myself with looking around me, and striving to appear as indifferent as possible, and as much used to all this splendor as if I had been born in it. But, to tell the truth, my head was almost dizzy with the strangeness of the sight, and the thought that I was really in London. What would my brother have said? What would Tom Legare, the treasurer of the Juvenile Temperance Society, have thought?

But I almost began to fancy I had no friends and relatives living in a little village three thousand five hundred miles off, in America; for it was hard to unite such a humble reminiscence with the splendid animation of the London-like scene around me.

And in the delirium of the moment, I began to indulge in foolish golden visions of the counts and countesses to whom Harry might introduce me; and every instant I expected to hear the waiters addressing some gentleman as 'My Lord', or 'Your Grace'. But if there were really any lords present, the waiters omitted their titles, at least in my hearing.

Mixed with these thoughts were confused visions of St Paul's and the Strand, which I determined to visit the very next morning, before breakfast, or perish in the attempt. And I even longed for Harry's return, that we might immediately sally out into the street, and see some of the sights, before the shops were all closed for the night.

While I thus sat alone, I observed one of the waiters eying me a little impertinently, as I thought, and as if he saw something queer about me. So I tried to assume a careless and lordly air, and by way of helping the thing, threw one leg over the other, like a young Prince Esterhazy; but all the time I felt my face burning with embarrassment, and for the time, I must have looked very guilty of something. But spite of this, I kept looking boldly out of my eyes, and straight through my blushes, and observed that every now and then little parties were made up among the gentlemen, and they retired into the rear of the house, as if going to a private apartment. And I over-heard one of them drop the word *Rouge*; but he could not have used rouge, for his face was exceedingly pale. Another said something about *Loo*.

At last Harry came back, his face rather flushed.

'Come along, Redburn,' said he.

So making no doubt we were off for a ramble, perhaps to Apsley House, in the Park, to get a sly peep at the old Duke before he retired for the night, for Harry had told me the Duke always went to bed early, I sprang up to follow him; but what was my disappointment and surprise, when he only led me into the passage, toward a staircase lighted by three marble Graces, unitedly holding a broad candelabra, like an elk's antlers, over the landing.

We rambled up the long, winding slope of those aristocratic stairs, every step of which, covered with Turkey rugs, looked gorgeous as the hammer-cloth of the Lord Mayor's coach; and Harry hied straight to a rosewood door, which, on magical hinges, sprang softly open to his touch.

As we entered the room, methought I was slowly sinking in some reluctant, sedgy sea; so thick and elastic the Persian carpeting, mimicking parterres of tulips, and roses, and jonquils, like a bower in Babylon.

Long lounges lay carelessly disposed, whose fine damask was interwoven, like the Gobelin tapestry, with pictorial tales of tilt and tourney. And oriental ottomans, whose cunning warp and woof were wrought into plaited serpents, undulating beneath beds of leaves, from which, here and there, they Aashed out sudden splendors of green scales and gold.

In the broad bay windows, as the hollows of King Charles' oaks, were Laocoon-like chairs, in the antique taste, draped with heavy fringes of bul-lion and silk. The walls, covered with a sort of tartan-French paper, varie-gated with bars of velvet, were hung round with mythological oil-paintings, suspended by tasseled cords of twisted silver and blue.

They were such pictures as the high-priests, for a bribe, showed to Alexander in the innermost shrine of the white temple in the Libyan oasis: such pictures as the pontiff of the sun strove to hide from Cortez, when, sword in hand, he burst open the sanctorum of the pyramid-fane at Cholula: such pictures as you may still see, perhaps, in the central alcove of the excavated mansion of Pansa, in Pompeii — in that part of it called by

Varro the hollow of the house: such pictures as Martial and Suetonius mention as being found in the private cabinet of the Emperor Tiberius: such pictures as are delineated on the bronze medals, to this day dug up on the ancient island of Capreæ: such pictures as you might have beheld in an arched recess, leading from the left hand of the secret side-gallery of the temple of Aphrodite in Corinth.

In the principal pier was a marble bracket, sculptured in the semblance of a dragon's crest, and supporting a bust, most wonderful to behold. It was that of a bald-headed old man, with a mysteriously-wicked expression, and imposing silence by one thin finger over his lips. His marble mouth seemed tremulous with secrets.

'Sit down, Wellingborough,' said Harry; 'don't be frightened, we are at home. — Ring the bell, will you? But stop;' — and advancing to the mysterious bust, he whispered something in its ear.

'He's a knowing mute, Wellingborough,' said he; 'who stays in this one place all the time, while he is yet running of errands. But mind you don't breathe any secrets in his ear.'

In obedience to a summons so singularly conveyed, to my amazement a servant almost instantly appeared, standing transfixed in the attitude of a bow.

'Cigars,' said Harry. When they came, he drew up a small table into the middle of the room, and lighting his cigar, bade me follow his example, and make myself happy.

Almost transported with such princely quarters, so undreamed of before, while leading my dog's life in the filthy forecastle of the Highlander, I twirled round a chair, and seated myself opposite my friend.

But all the time, I felt ill at heart; and was filled with an under current of dismal forebodings. But I strove to dispel them; and turning to my companion, exclaimed, 'And pray, do you live here, Harry, in this Palace of Aladdin?'

'Upon my soul,' he cried, 'you have hit it: — you must have been here before! Aladdin's Palace! Why, Wellingborough, it goes by that very name.'

Then he laughed strangely: and for the first time, I thought he had been quaffing too freely: yet, though he looked wildly from his eyes, his general carriage was firm.

'Who are you looking at so hard, Wellingborough?' said he.

'I am afraid, Harry,' said I, 'that when you left me just now, you must have been drinking something stronger than wine.'

'Hear him now,' said Harry, turning round, as if addressing the bald-headed bust on the bracket, — 'a parson 'pon honor! — But remark you, Wellingborough, my boy, I must leave you again, and for a considerably longer time than before: — I may not be back again to-night.'

'What?' said I.

'Be still,' he cried,'hear me, I know the old duke here, and —'

'Who? not the Duke of Wellington,' said I, wondering whether Harry was really going to include *him* too, in his long list of confidential friends and acquaintances.

'Pooh!' cried Harry, 'I mean the white-whiskered old man you saw below; they called *the Duke*: — he keeps the house. I say, I know him well, and he knows *me*; and he knows what brings me here, also. Well; we have arranged every thing about you; you are to stay in this room, and sleep here to-night, and — and —' continued he, speaking low — 'you must guard this letter —' slipping a sealed one into my hand — 'and, if I am not back by morning, you must post right on to Bury, and leave the letter there; — here, take this paper — it's all set down here in black and white — where you are to go, and what you are to do. And after that's done — mind, this is all in case I don't return — then you may do what you please: stay here in London awhile, or go back to Liverpool. And here's enough to pay all your expenses.'

All this was a thunder stroke. I thought Harry was crazy. I held the purse in my motionless hand, and stared at him, till the tears almost started from my eyes.

'What's the matter, Redburn?' he cried, with a wild sort of laugh — 'you are not afraid of me, are you? — No, no! I believe in you, my boy, or you would not hold that purse in your hand; no, nor that letter.'

'What in heaven's name do you mean?' at last I exclaimed, 'you don't really intend to desert me in this strange place, do you, Harry?' and I snatched him by the hand.

'Pooh, pooh,' he cried, 'let me go. I tell you, it's all right: do as I say: that's all. Promise me now, will you? Swear it! — no, no,' he added, vehemently, as I conjured him to tell me more — 'no, I won't: I have nothing more to tell you — not a word. Will you swear?'

'But one sentence more for your own sake, Harry: hear me!'

'Not a syllable! Will you swear? — you will not? then here, give me that purse: — there — there — take that — and that — and that; — that will pay your fare back to Liverpool; good-by to you: you are not my friend,' and he wheeled round his back.

I know not what flashed through my mind, but something suddenly impelled me; and grasping his hand, I swore to him what he demanded.

Immediately he ran to the bust, whispered a word, and the white-whiskered old man appeared: whom he clapped on the shoulder, and then introduced me as his friend — young Lord Stormont; and bade the almond tree look wed to the comforts of his lordship, while he — Harry — was gone.

The almond tree blandly bowed, and grimaced, with a peculiar expression, that I hated on the spot. After a few words more, he withdrew. Harry then shook my hand heartily, and without giving me a chance to say one word, seized his cap, and darted out of the room, saying, 'Leave not this room to-night; and remember the letter, and Bury!'

I fell into a chair, and gazed round at the strange-looking walls and mysterious pictures, and up to the chandelier at the ceiling; then rose, and opened the door, and looked down the lighted passage; but only heard the hum from the roomful below, scattered voices, and a hushed ivory rattling from the closed apartments adjoining. I stepped back into the room, and a terrible revulsion came over me; I would have given the world had I been safe back in Liverpool, fast asleep in my old bunk in Prince's Dock.

I shuddered at every footfall, and almost thought it must be some assassin pursuing me. The whole place seemed infected; and a strange thought came over me, that in the very damasks around, some eastern plague had been imported. And was that pale yellow wine, that I drank below, drugged? thought I. This must be some house whose foundations take hold on the pit. But these fearful reveries only enchanted me fast to my chair; so that, though I then wished to rush forth from the house, my limbs seemed manacled. While thus chained to my seat, something seemed suddenly flung open; a confused sound of imprecations, mixed with the ivory rattling, louder than before, burst upon my ear, and through the partly open door of the room where I was, I caught sight of a tall, frantic man, with clenched hands, wildly darting through the passage, toward the stairs.

And all the while, Harry ran through my soul — in and out, at every door, that burst open to his vehement rush.

At that moment my whole acquaintance with him passed like lightning through my mind, till I asked myself why he had come here, to London, to do this thing? — why would not Liverpool have answered? and what did he want of me? But, every way, his conduct was unaccountable.

From the hour he had accosted me on board the ship, his manner seemed gradually changed; and from the moment we had sprung into the cab, he had seemed almost another person from what he had seemed before,

But what could I do? He was gone, that was certain; — would he ever come back? But he might still be somewhere in the house; and with a shudder, I thought of that ivory rattling, and was almost ready to dart forth, search every room, and save him. But that would be madness, and I had sworn not to do so. There seemed nothing left, but to await his return. Yet, if he did not return, what then? I took out the purse, and counted over the money, and looked at the letter and paper of memoranda.

Though I vividly remember it all, I will not give the superscription of the letter, nor the contents of the paper. But after I had looked at them attentively, and considered that Harry could have no conceivable object in deceiving me, I thought to myself, Yes, he's in earnest; and here I am — yes, even in London! And here in this room will I stay, come what will. I will implicitly follow his directions, and so see out the last of this thing.

But spite of these thoughts, and spite of the metropolitan magnificence around me, I was mysteriously alive to a dreadful feeling, which I had never before felt, except when penetrating into the lowest and most squalid haunts of sailor iniquity in Liverpool. All the mirrors and marbles around me seemed crawling over with lizards; and I thought to myself, that though gilded and golden, the serpent of vice is a serpent still.

It was now grown very late; and faint with excitement, I threw myself upon a lounge; but for some time tossed about restless, in a sort of nightmare. Every few moments, spite of my oath, I was upon the point of starting up, and rushing into the street, to inquire where I was; but remembering Harry's injunctions, and my own ignorance of the town, and that it was now so late, I again tried to be composed.

At last, I fell asleep, dreaming about Harry fighting a duel of dice-boxes with the military-looking man below; and the next thing I knew, was the glare of a light before my eyes, and Harry himself, very pale, stood before me.

'The letter and paper,' he cried.

I fumbled in my pockets, and handed them to him.

'There! there! there! thus I tear you,' he cried, wrenching the letter to pieces with both hands like a madman, and stamping upon the fragments. 'I am off for America; the game is up.'

'For God's sake explain,' said I, now utterly bewildered, and frightened.' Tell me, Harry, what is it? You have not been gambling?'

'Ha, ha,' he deliriously laughed. 'Gambling? red and white, you mean? — cards? — dice? — the bones? — Ha, ha! — Gambling? gambling?' he ground out between his teeth — 'what two devilish, stiletto-sounding syllables they are!'

'Wellingborough,' he added, marching up to me slowly, but with his eyes blazing into mine — 'Wellingborough' — and fumbling in his breastpocket, he drew forth a dirk — 'Here, Wellingborough, take it — take it, I say — are you stupid? — there, there' — and he pushed it into my hands. 'Keep it away from me — keep it out of my sight — I don't want it near me, while I feel as I do. They serve suicides scurvily here, Wellingborough; they don't bury them decently. See that bell-rope! By Heaven, it's an invitation to hang myself' — and seizing it by the gilded handle at the end, he twitched it down from the wall.

'In God's name, what ails you?' I cried.

'Nothing, oh nothing,' said Harry, now assuming a treacherous, tropical calmness — 'nothing, Redburn; nothing in the world. I'm the serenest of men.'

'But give me that dirk,' he suddenly cried — 'let me have it, I say. Oh! I don't mean to murder myself — I'm past that now — give it me' — and snatching it from my hand, he flung down an empty purse, and with a terrific stab, nailed it fast with the dirk to the table.

'There now,' he cried, 'there's something for the old duke to see to-morrow morning; that's about all that's left of me — that's my skeleton, Wellingborough. But come, don't be down-hearted; there's a little more gold yet in Golconda; I have a guinea or two left. Don't stare so, my boy; we shall be in Liverpool to-morrow night; we start in the morning' — and turning his back, he began to whistle very fiercely.

'And this, then,' said I, 'is your showing me London, is it, Harry? I did not think this; but tell me your secret, whatever it is, and I will not regret not seeing the town.'

He turned round upon me like lghtning, and cried, 'Redburn! you must swear another oath, and instantly.

'And why?' said I, in alarm, 'what more would you have me swear?'

'Never to question me again about this infernal trip to London!' he shouted, with the foam at his lips — 'never to breathe it! swear!'

'I certainly shall not trouble you, Harry, with questions, if you do not desire it,' said I, 'but there's no need of swearing.

'Swear it, I say, as you love me, Redburn,' he added, imploringly.

'Well, then, I solemnly do. Now lie down, and let us forget ourselves as soon as we can; for me, you have made me the most miserable dog alive.'

'And what am I?' cried Harry; 'but pardon me, Redburn, I did not mean to offend; if you knew all — but no, no! — never mind, never mind!' And he ran to the bust, and whispered in its ear. A waiter came.

'Brandy,' whispered Harry, with clenched teeth.

'Are you not going to sleep, then?' said I, more and more alarmed at his wildness, and fearful of the effects of his drinking still more, in such a mood.

'No sleep for me! sleep if *you* can — I mean to sit up with a decanter! — let me see' — looking at the ormolu clock on the mantle — 'it's only two hours to morning.'

The waiter, looking very sleepy, and with a green shade on his brow, appeared with the decanter and glasses on a salver, and was told to leave it and depart.

Seeing that Harry was not to be moved, I once more threw myself on the lounge. I did not sleep; but, like a somnambulist, only dozed now and then; starting from my dreams; while Harry sat, with his hat on, at the table; the brandy before him; from which he occasionally poured into his glass. Instead of exciting him, however, to my amazement, the spirits seemed to soothe him down; and, ere long, he was comparatively calm.

At last, just as I had fallen into a deep sleep, I was wakened by his shaking me, and saying our cab was at the door.

'Look! it is broad day,' said he, brushing aside the heavy hangings of the window.

We left the room; and passing through the now silent and deserted hall of pillars, which, at this hour, reeked as with blended roses and cigar-stumps decayed; a dumb waiter, rubbing his eyes, hung open the street door; we sprung into the cab; and soon found ourselves whirled along north-ward by railroad, toward Prince's Dock and the Highlander.

Behold The Organ

This excerpt from the novel Redburn *continues the saga of Redburn and Bolton, who has joined the ship's crew. A new character is introduced, a beautiful young boy named Carlo. On board, Carlos entertains the sailors by playing the "hand organ." This seems to me to be Melville in his "high camp" mode. As in the sperm scene in* Moby Dick, *Melville seems to revel in an extended* double entendre.

This excerpt contains a portion of chapter 49 of the novel; however there are no omissions in the selection excerpted. The title is contained within Melville's text, but is not his title for the chapter.

There was on board our ship, among the emigrant passengers, a rich-cheeked, chestnut-haired Italian boy, arrayed in a faded, olive-hued velvet jacket, and tattered trowsers rolled up to his knee. He was not above fifteen years of age; but in the twilight pensiveness of his full morning eyes, there seemed to sleep experiences so sad and various, that his days must have seemed to him years. It was not an eye like Harry's tho' Harry's was larger and womanly. It shone with a soft and spiritual radiance, like a moist star in a tropic sky; and spoke of humility, deep-seated thoughtfulness, yet a careless endurance of all the ills of life.

The head was if any thing small; and heaped with thick clusters of tendril curls, half overhanging the brows and delicate ears, it somehow reminded you of a classic vase, piled up with Falernian foliage.

From the knee downward, the naked leg was beautiful to behold as any lady's arm; so soft and rounded, with infantile ease and grace. His whole figure was free, fine, and indolent; he was such a boy as might have ripened into life in a Neapolitan vineyard; such a boy as gipsies steal in infancy; such a boy as Murillo often painted, when he went among the poor and outcast, for subjects wherewith to captivate the eyes of rank and wealth; such a boy, as only Andalusian beggars are, full of poetry, gushing from every rent.

Carlo was his name; a poor and friendless son of earth, who had no sire; and on life's ocean was swept along, as spoon-drift in a gale.

Some months previous, he had landed in Prince's Dock, with his hand-organ, from a Messina vessel; and had walked the streets of Liverpool, playing the sunny airs of southern climes, among the northern fog and drizzle. And now, having laid by enough to pay his passage over the Atlantic, he had again embarked, to seek his fortunes in America.

From the first, Harry took to the boy.

"Carlo," said Harry, "how did you succeed in England?"

He was reclining upon an old sail spread on the long-boat; and throwing back his soiled but tasseled cap, and caressing one leg like a child, he looked up, and said in his broken English — that seemed like mixing the potent wine of Oporto with some delicious syrup: — said he, "Ah! I succeed very well! — for I have tunes for the young and the old, the gay and the sad. I have marches for military young men, and love-airs for the ladies, and solemn sounds for the aged. I never draw a crowd, but I know from their faces what airs will best please them; I never stop before a house, but I judge from its portico for what tune they will soonest toss me some silver. And I ever play sad airs to the merry, and merry airs to the sad; and most always the rich best fancy the sad, and the poor the merry."

"But do you not sometimes meet with cross and crabbed old men," said Harry, "who would much rather have your room than your music?"

"Yes, sometimes," said Carlo, playing with his foot, "sometimes I do."

"And then, knowing the value of quiet to unquiet men, I suppose you never leave them under a shilling?"

"No," continued the boy, "I love my organ as I do myself, for it is my only friend, poor organ! it sings to me when I am sad, and cheers me; and I never play before a house, on purpose to be paid for leaving off, not I; would I, poor organ?" — looking down the hatchway where it was. "No, that I never have done, and never will do, though I starve; for when people drive me away, I do not think my organ is to blame, but they themselves are to blame; for such people's musical pipes are cracked, and grown rusted, that no more music can be breathed into their souls."

"No, Carlo; no music like yours, perhaps," said Harry, with a laugh.

"Ah! there's the mistake. Though my organ is as full of melody, as a hive is of bees; yet no organ can make music in unmusical breasts; no more than my native winds can, when they breathe upon a harp without chords."

Next day was a serene and delightful one; and in the evening when the vessel was just rippling along impelled by a gentle yet steady breeze, and the poor emigrants, relieved from their late sufferings, were gathered on deck; Carlo suddenly started up from his lazy reclinings; went below, and, assisted by the emigrants, returned with his organ.

Now, music is a holy thing, and its instruments, however humble, are to be loved and revered. Whatever has made, or does make, or may make music, should be held sacred as the golden bridle-bit of the Shah of Persia's horse, and the golden hammer, with which his hoofs are shod. Musical instruments should be like the silver tongs, with which the high-priests tended the Jewish altars — never to be touched by a hand profane. Who would bruise the poorest reed of Pan, though plucked from a beggar's hedge, would insult the melodious god himself.

And there is no humble thing with music in it, not a fife, not a negro-fiddle, that is not to be reverenced as much as the grandest architectural organ that ever rolled its flood-tide of harmony down a cathedral nave. For even a Jew's-harp may be so played, as to awaken all the fairies that are in us, and make them dance in our souls, as on a moon-lit sward of violets.

But what subtle power is this, residing in but a bit of steel, which might have made a tenpenny nail, that so enters, without knocking, into our inmost beings, and shows us all hidden things?

Not in a spirit of foolish speculation altogether, in no merely transcendental mood, did the glorious Greek of old fancy the human soul to be essentially a harmony. And if we grant that theory of Paracelsus and Campanella, that every man has four souls within him; then can we account for those banded sounds with silver links, those quartettes of melody, that sometimes sit and sing within us, as if our souls were baronial halls, and our music were made by the hoarest old harpers of Wales.

But look! here is poor Carlo's organ; and while the silent crowd surrounds him, there he stands, looking mildly but inquiringly about him; his right hand pulling and twitching the ivory knobs at one end of his instrument.

Behold the organ!

Surely, if much virtue lurk in the old fiddles of Cremona, and if their melody be in proportion to their antiquity, what divine ravishments may we not anticipate from this venerable, embrowned old organ, which might almost have played the Dead March in Saul, when King Saul himself was buried.

A fine old organ! carved into fantastic old towers, and turrets, and belfries; its architecture seems somewhat of the Gothic, monastic order; in front, it looks like the West-Front of York Minster.

What sculptured arches, leading into mysterious intricacies! — what mullioned windows, that seem as if they must look into chapels flooded with devotional sunsets! — what flying buttresses, and gable-ends, and niches with saints! — But stop! 'tis a Moorish iniquity; for here, as I live, is a Saracenic arch; which, for aught I know, may lead into some interior

Alhambra.

Ay, it does; for as Carlo now turns his hand, I hear the gush of the Fountain of Lions, as he plays some thronged Italian air — a mixed and liquid sea of sound, that dashes its spray in my face.

Play on, play on, Italian boy! what though the notes be broken, here's that within that mends them. Turn hither your pensive, morning eyes; and while I list to the organs twain — one yours, one mine — let me gaze fathoms down into thy fathomless eye; — 'tis good as gazing down into the great South Sea, and seeing the dazzling rays of the dolphins there.

Play on, play on! for to every note come trooping, now, triumphant standards, armies marching — all the pomp of sound. Methinks I am Xerxes, the nucleus of the martial neigh of all the Persian studs. Like gilded damask-flies, thick clustering on some lofty bough, my satraps swarm around me.

But now the pageant passes, and I droop; while Carlo taps his ivory knobs; and plays some flute-like saraband — soft, dulcet, dropping sounds, like silver cans in bubbling brooks. And now a clanging, martial air, as if ten thousand brazen trumpets, forged from spurs and sword-hilts, called North, and South, and East, to rush to West!

Again — what blasted heath is this? — what goblin sounds of Macbeth's witches? — Beethoven's Spirit Waltz! the muster-call of sprites and specters. Now come, hands joined, Medusa, Hecate, she of Endor, and all the Blocksberg's, demons dire.

Once more the ivory knobs are tapped; and long-drawn, golden sounds are heard — some ode to Cleopatra; slowly loom, and solemnly expand, vast, rounding orbs of beauty; and before me float innumerable queens, deep dipped in silver gauzes.

All this could Carlo do — make, unmake me; build me up; to pieces take me; and join me limb to limb. He is the architect of domes of sound, and bowers of song.

And all is done with that old organ! Reverenced, then, be all street organs; more melody is at the beck of my Italian boy, than lurks in squadrons of Parisian orchestras.

But look! Carlo has that to feast the eye as well as ear; and the same wondrous magic in me, magnifies them into grandeur; though every figure greatly needs the artist's repairing hand, and sadly needs a dusting.

A Secret Have I;
Let Me Whisper It To Thee Aside;
In This Closet

*Pierre has long been the bugaboo among Melville's novels. The inces-
tuous themes of the novel outraged Melville's contemporaries; the novel has
not yet recovered from the critical drubbing it initially received.*

*In this novel Melville turned, for the first in his career, away from an
all-male (or predominantly male) society. Here, he looks at the American
family. And what a family it is: the mother is in love with the son, the son
has a habit of retiring to his closet and masturbating to a picture of his
father, the same son eventually falls in love with his sister (!) because she
reminds him so much of his father. No wonder the novel shocked the reading
public of the time; the only question is whether the incestuous ménage-a-trois
shocked more for being incestuous or bisexual.*

*In these post-Freudian times, the novel is less likely to scandalize. In
fact, the psychological underpinnings are fascinating when one realizes that
Melville uncovered the sexual undertones of the family dynamic some fifty
years before Freud.*

*In the selection, Pierre retires to his closet. He goes into a trance star-
ing at a portrait of his father which captures a lusty expression on the man's
face — needless to say, it's a portrait his mother cannot abide. Note how
Melville describes the pleasures of the closet.*

The excerpt below starts from chapter Book IV.

In the cold courts of justice the dull head demands oaths, and holy
writ proofs; but in the warm halls of the heart one single, untestified
memory's spark shall suffice to enkindle such a blaze of evidence, that all
the corners of conviction are as suddenly lighted up as a midnight city by a
burning building, which on every side whirls its reddened brands.

In a locked, rounded-windowed closet connecting with the chamber
of Pierre, and whither he had always been wont to go, in those sweetly
awful hours, when the spirit crieth to the spirit, Come into solitude with
me, twin-brother; come away: a secret have I; let me whisper it to thee
aside; in this closet, sacred to the Tadmor privacies and repose of the some-

times solitary Pierre, there hung, by long cords from the cornice, a small portrait in oil, before which Pierre had many a time trancedly stood. Had this painting hung in any annual public exhibition, and in its turn been described in print by the casual glancing critics, they would probably have described it thus, and truthfully: "An impromptu portrait of a fine-looking, gay-hearted, youthful gentleman. He is lightly, and, as it were, airily and but grazingly seated in, or rather flittingly tenanting an old-fashioned chair of Malacca. One arm confining his hat and cane is loungingly thrown over the back of the chair, while the fingers of the other hand play with his gold watch-seal and key. The free-templed head is sideways turned, with a peculiarly bright, and care-free, morning expression. He seems as if just dropped in for a visit upon some familiar acquaintance. Altogether, the painting is exceedingly clever and cheerful; with a fine, off-handed expression about it. Undoubtedly a portrait, and no fancy-piece; and, to hazard a vague conjecture, by an amateur."

So bright, and so cheerful then; so trim, and so young; so singularly healthful, and handsome; what subtile element could so steep this whole portrait, that, to the wife of the original, it was namelessly unpleasant and repelling? The mother of Pierre could never abide this picture which she had always asserted did signally belie her husband. Her fond memories of the departed refused to hang one single wreath around it. It is not he, she would emphatically and almost indignantly exclaim, when more urgently besought to reveal the cause for so unreasonable a dissent from the opinion of nearly all the other connections and relatives of the deceased. But the portrait which she held to do justice to her husband, correctly to convey his features in detail, and more especially their truest, and finest, and noblest combined expression; this portrait was a much larger one, and in the great drawing-room below occupied the most conspicuous and honorable place on the wall.

Even to Pierre these two paintings had always seemed strangely dissimilar. And as the larger one had been painted many years after the other, and therefore brought the original pretty nearly within his own childish recollections; therefore, he himself could not but deem it by far the more truthful and life-like presentation of his father. So that the mere preference of his mother, however strong, was not at all surprising to him, but rather coincided with his own conceit. Yet not for this, must the other portrait be so decidedly rejected. Because, in the first place, there was a difference in time, and some difference of costume to be considered, and the wide difference of the styles of the respective artists, and the wide difference of those respective, semi-reflected, ideal faces, which, even in the presence of the original, a spiritual artist will rather choose to draw from than from the fleshy face, however brilliant and fine. Moreover, while the larger portrait was that of a middle-aged, married man, and seemed to possess all the nameless and slightly portly tranquillities, incident to that condition when a felicitous one; the smaller portrait painted a brisk, unentangled, young bachelor, gayly ranging up and down in the world; light-hearted, and a very little bladish perhaps; and charged to the lips with the first uncloying morning fullness and freshness of life. Here, certainly, large allowance was to be made in any careful, candid estimation of these portraits. To Pierre this conclusion had become well-nigh irresistible, when he placed side by side two portraits of himself; one taken in his early childhood, a frocked and belted boy of four years old; and the other, a grown youth of sixteen. Except an indestructible, all-surviving something in the eyes and on the temples, Pierre could hardly recognize the loud-laughing boy in the tall, and pensively smiling youth. If a few years, then, can have in *me* made all this difference, why not in my father? thought Pierre.

Besides all this, Pierre considered the history, and, so to speak, the family legend of the smaller painting. In his fifteenth year, it was made a present to him by an old maiden aunt, who resided in the city, and who cherished the memory of Pierre's father, with all that wonderful amaranthine devotion which an advanced maiden sister ever feels for the idea of a beloved younger brother, now dead and irrevocably gone. As the only child of that brother, Pierre was an object of the warmest and most extravagant attachment on the part of this lonely aunt, who seemed to see, transformed into youth once again, the likeness, and very soul of her brother, in the fair, inheriting brow of Pierre. Though the portrait we speak of was inordinately prized by her, yet at length the strict canon of her romantic and imaginative love asserted the portrait to be Pierre's—for Pierre was not only his father's only child, but his namesake—so soon as Pierre should be old enough to value aright so holy and inestimable a treasure. She had accordingly sent it to him, trebly boxed, and finally covered with a waterproof cloth; and it was delivered at Saddle Meadows, by an express, confidential messenger, an old gentleman of leisure, once her forlorn, because rejected gallant, but now her contented, and chatty neighbor. Henceforth, before a gold-framed and gold-lidded ivory miniature,—a fraternal gift— Aunt Dorothea now offered up her morning and her evening rites, to the memory of the noblest and handsomest of brothers. Yet an annual visit to the far closet of Pierre—no slight undertaking now for one so stricken in years, and every way infirm—attested the earnestness of that strong sense of duty, that painful renunciation of self, which had induced her I voluntarily to part with the precious memorial.

"Tell me, aunt," the child Pierre had early said to her, long before the portrait became his—"tell me, aunt, how this chair-portrait, as you call it, was painted;—who painted it?—whose chair was this?—have you the chair now?—I don't see it in your room here;—what is papa looking at so strangely?—I should like to know now, what papa was thinking of, then. Do, now, dear aunt, tell me all about this picture, so that when it is mine, as you promise me, I shall know its whole history."

"Sit down, then, and be very still and attentive, my dear child," said Aunt Dorothea; while she a little averted her head, and tremulously and inaccurately sought her pocket, till little Pierre cried—"Why, aunt, the story of the picture is not in any little book, is it, that you are going to take out and read to me?"

"My handkerchief, my child."

"Why, aunt, here it is, at your elbow; here, on the table; here, aunt; take it, do. Oh, don't tell me any thing about the picture, now; I won't hear it."

"Be still, my darling Pierre," said his aunt, taking the handkerchief, "draw the curtain a little, dearest; the light hurts my eyes. Now, go into the closet, and bring me my dark shawl;—take your time.—There; thank you, Pierre; now sit down again, and I will begin.—The picture was painted long ago, my child; you were not born then."

"Not born?" cried little Pierre.

"Not born," said his aunt.

"Well, go on, aunt; but don't tell me again that once upon a time I was not little Pierre at all, and yet my father was alive. Go on, aunt,—do, do!"

"Why, how nervous you are getting, my child;—Be patient; I am very old, Pierre; and old people never like to be hurried."

"Now, my own dear Aunt Dorothea, do forgive me this once, and go on with your story."

"When your poor father was quite a young man, my child, and was on one of his long autumnal visits to his friends in this city, he was rather intimate at times with a cousin of his, Ralph Winwood, who was about his own age,—a fine youth he was, too, Pierre."

"I never saw him, aunt; pray, where is he now?" interrupted Pierre;—

"does he live in the country, now, as mother and I do?"

"Yes, my child; but a far-away, beautiful country, I hope; he's in heaven, I trust."

"Dead," sighed little Pierre—"go on, aunt."

"Now, cousin Ralph had a great love for painting, my child; and he spent many hours in a room, hung all round with pictures and portraits; and there he had his easel and brushes; and much liked to paint his friends, and hang their faces on his walls; so that when all alone by himself, he yet had plenty of company, who always wore their best expressions to him, and never once ruffled him, by ever getting cross or ill-natured, little Pierre. Often, he had besought your father to sit to him; saying, that his silent circle of friends would never be complete, till your father consented to join them. But in those days, my child, your father was always in motion. It was hard for me to get him to stand still, while I tied his cravat; for he never came to any one but me for that. So he was always putting off, and putting off cousin Ralph. 'Some other time, cousin; not to-day;—to-morrow, perhaps;—or next week;'— and so, at last cousin Ralph began to despair. But I'll catch him yet, cried sly cousin Ralph. So now he said nothing more to your father about the matter of painting him; but every pleasant morning kept his easel and brushes and every thing in readiness; so as to be ready the first moment your father should chance to drop in upon him from his long strolls; for it was now and then your father's wont to pay flying little visits to cousin Ralph in his painting-room.—But, my child, you may draw back the curtain now—it's getting very dim here, seems to me."

"Well, I thought so all along, aunt," said little Pierre, obeying; "but didn't you say the light hurt your eyes."

"But it does not now, little Pierre."

"Well, well; go on, go on, aunt; you can't think how interested I am," said little Pierre, drawing his stool close up to the quilted satin hem of his good Aunt Dorothea's dress.

"I will, my child. But first let me tell you, that about this time there arrived in the port, a cabin-full of French emigrants of quality;—poor people, Pierre, who were forced to fly from their native land, because of the cruel, blood-shedding times there. But you have read all that in the little history I gave you, a good while ago."

"I know all about it;—the French Revolution," said little Pierre.

"What a famous little scholar you are, my dear child,"— said Aunt Dorothea, faintly smiling—"among those poor, but noble emigrants, there was a beautiful young girl, whose sad fate afterward made a great noise in the city, and made many eyes to weep, but in vain, for she never was heard of any more."

"How? how? aunt;—I don't understand;—did she disappear then, aunt?"

"I was a little before my story, child. Yes, she did disappear, and never was heard of again; but that was afterward, some time afterward, my child. I am very sure it was; I could take my oath of that, Pierre."

"Why, dear aunt," said little Pierre, "how earnestly you talk—after what? your voice is getting very strange; do now;—don't talk that way; you frighten me so, aunt."

"Perhaps it is this bad cold I have to-day; it makes my voice a little hoarse, I fear, Pierre. But I will try and not talk so hoarsely again. Well, my child, some time before this beautiful young lady disappeared, indeed it was only shortly after the poor emigrants landed, your father made her acquaintance; and with many other humane gentlemen of the city, provided for the wants of the strangers, for they were very poor indeed, having been stripped of every thing, save a little trifling jewelry, which could not go very far. At last, the friends of your father endeavored to dissuade him from visiting these people so much; they were fearful that as the young lady was so very beautiful, and a little inclined to be intriguing—so some said—your father might be tempted to marry her; which would not have been a wise thing in him; for though the young lady might have been very beautiful, and good-hearted, yet no one on this side the water certainly knew her history; and she was a foreigner; and would not have made so suitable and excellent a match for your father as your dear mother afterward did, my child. But, for myself, I—who always knew your father very well in all his intentions, and he was very confidential with me, too—I, for my part, never credited that he would do so unwise a thing as marry the strange young lady. At any rate, he at last discontinued his visits to the emigrants; and it was after this that the young lady disappeared. Some said that she must have voluntarily but secretly returned into her own country; and others declared that she must have been kidnapped by French emissaries; for, after her disappearance, rumor began to hint that she was of the noblest birth, and some ways allied to the royal family; and then, again, there were some who shook their heads darkly, and muttered of drownings, and other dark things; which one always hears hinted when people disappear, and no one can find them. But though your father and many other gentlemen moved heaven and earth to find trace of her, yet, as I said before, my child, she never re-appeared."

"The poor French lady!" sighed little Pierre. "Aunt, I'm afraid she was murdered."

"Poor lady, there is no telling," said his aunt. "But listen, for I am coming to the picture again. Now, at the time your father was so often visiting the emigrants, my child, cousin Ralph was one of those who a little fancied that your father was courting her; but cousin Ralph being a quiet young man, and a scholar, not well acquainted with what is wise, or what is foolish in the great world; cousin Ralph would not have been at all morti-fied had your father really wedded with the refugee young lady. So vainly thinking, as I told you, that your father was courting her, he fancied it would be a very fine thing if he could paint your father as her wooer; that is, paint him just after his coming from his daily visits to the emigrants. So he watched his chance; every thing being ready in his painting-room, as I told you be-fore; and one morning, sure enough, in dropt your father from his walk. But before he came into the room, cousin Ralph had spied him from the window; and when your father entered, cousin Ralph had the sitting-chair ready drawn out, back of his easel, but still fronting toward him, and pre-tended to he very busy painting. He said to your father—'Glad to see you, cousin Pierre; I am just about something here; sit right down there now, and tell me the news; and I'll sally out with you presently. And tell us some-thing of the emigrants, cousin Pierre,' he slyly added—wishing, you see, to get your father's thoughts running that supposed wooing way, so that he might catch some sort of corresponding expression you see, little Pierre."

"I don't know that I precisely understand, aunt; but go on, I am so interested; do go on, dear aunt."

"Well, by many little cunning shifts and contrivances, cousin Ralph kept your father there sitting, and sitting in the chair, rattling and rattling away, and so self-forgetful too, that he never heeded that all the while sly cousin Ralph was painting and painting just as fast as ever he could; and only making believe to laugh at your father's wit; in short, cousin Ralph was stealing his portrait, my child."

"Not *stealing* it, I hope," said Pierre, "that would be very wicked."

"Well, then, we won't call it stealing, since I am sure that cousin Ralph kept your father all the time off from him, and so, could not have possibly picked his pocket, though indeed, he slyly picked his portrait, so to speak. And if indeed it was stealing, or any thing of that sort; yet seeing how much comfort that portrait has been to me, Pierre, and how much it will yet be to you, I hope; I think we must very heartily forgive cousin Ralph, for what he then did."

"Yes, I think we must indeed," chimed in little Pierre, now eagerly eying the very portrait in question, which hung over the mantle.

"Well, by catching your father two or three times more in that way, cousin Ralph at last finished the painting; and when it was all framed, and every way completed, he would have surprised your father by hanging it boldly up in his room among his other portraits, had not your father one morning suddenly come to him—while, indeed, the very picture itself was placed face down on a table and cousin Ralph fixing the cord to it—came to him, and frightened cousin Ralph by quietly saying, that now that he thought of it, it seemed to him that cousin Ralph had been playing tricks with him; but he hoped it was not so. 'What do you mean?' said cousin Ralph, a little flurried. 'You have not been hanging my portrait up here, have you, cousin Ralph?' said your father, glancing along the walls. 'I'm glad I don't see it. It is my whim, cousin Ralph,—and perhaps it is a very silly one,—but if you have been lately painting my portrait, I want you to destroy it; at any rate, don't show it to any one, keep it out of sight. What's that you have there, cousin Ralph?'

"Cousin Ralph was now more and more fluttered; not knowing what to make—as indeed, to this day, I don't completely myself—of your father's strange manner. But he rallied, and said—'This, cousin Pierre, is a secret portrait I have here; you must be aware that we portrait-painters are sometimes called upon to paint such. I, therefore, can not show it to you, or tell you any thing about it.'

"'Have you been painting my portrait or not, cousin Ralph?' said your father, very suddenly and pointedly.

"'I have painted nothing that looks as you there look,' said cousin Ralph, evasively, observing in your father's face a fierce-like expression, which he had never seen there before. And more than that, your father could not get from him."

"And what then?" said little Pierre.

"Why not much, my child; only your father never so much as caught one glimpse of that picture; indeed, never knew for certain, whether there was such a painting in the world. Cousin Ralph secretly gave it to me, knowing how tenderly I loved your father; making me solemnly promise never to expose it anywhere where your father could ever see it, or any way hear of it. This promise I faithfully kept; and it was only after your dear father's death, that I hung it in my chamber. There, Pierre, you now have the story of the chair-portrait."

"And a very strange one it is," said Pierre—"and so interesting, I shall never forget it, aunt."

"I hope you never will, my child. Now ring the bell, and we will have a little fruit-cake, and I will take a glass of wine, Pierre;—do you hear, my child?—the bell—ring it. Why, what do you do standing there, Pierre?"

Why didn't papa want to have cousin Ralph paint his picture, aunt?" "How these children's minds do ran!" exclaimed old Aunt Dorothea staring at little Pierre in amazement—"That indeed is more than I can tell you, little Pierre. But cousin Ralph had a foolish fancy about it. He used to tell me, that being in your father's room some few days after the last scene I described, he noticed there a very wonderful work on Physiognomy, as they call it, in which the strangest and shadowiest rules were laid down for detecting people's innermost secrets by studying their faces. And so, foolish cousin Ralph always flattered himself, that the reason your father did not want his portrait taken was, because he was secretly in love with the French young lady, and did not want his secret published in a portrait; since the wonderful work on Physiognomy had, as it were, indirectly warned him against running that risk. But cousin Ralph being such a retired and solitary sort of a youth, he always had such curious whimsies about things. For my part, I don't believe your father ever had any such ridiculous ideas on the subject. To be sure, I myself can not tell you *why* he did not want his picture taken; but when you get to be as old as I am, little Pierre, you will find that every one, even the best of us, at times, is apt to act very queerly and unaccountably; indeed some things we do, we can not entirely explain the reason of, even to ourselves, little Pierre. But you will know all about these strange matters by-and-by."

"I hope I shall, aunt," said little Pierre.—"But, dear aunt, I thought Marten was to bring in some fruit-cake?" "Ring the bell for him, then, my child." "Oh! I forgot," said little Pierre, doing her bidding. By-and-by, while the aunt was sipping her wine; and the boy eating his cake, and both their eyes were fixed on the portrait in question; little Pierre, pushing his stool nearer the picture exclaimed—"Now, aunt, did papa really look exactly like that? Did you see him in that. same buff vest, and huge-figured neckcloth? I remember the seal and key, pretty well; and it was only a week ago that I saw mamma take them out of a little locked drawer in her wardrobe—but I don't remember the queer whiskers; nor the buff vest; nor the huge white-figured neckcloth; did you ever see papa in that very neckcloth, aunt?"

"My child, it was I that chose the stuff for that neckcloth; yes, and hemmed it for him, and worked P.O. in one corner; but that ain't in the picture. It is an excellent likeness, my child, neckcloth and all; as he looked at that time. Why, little Pierre, sometimes I sit here all alone by myself, and gazing, and gazing, and gazing at that face, till I begin to think your father is looking at me, and smiling at me, and nodding at me, and saying— Dorothea! Dorothea!"

"How strange," said little Pierre, "I think it begins to look at me now, aunt. Hark! aunt, it's so silent all round in this old-fashioned room, that I think I hear a little jingling in the picture, as if the watch-seal was striking against the key— Hark! aunt."

"Bless me, don't talk so strangely, my child." "I heard mamma say once—but she did not say so to me— that, for her part, she did not like Aunt Dorothea's picture; it was not a good likeness, so she said. Why don't mamma like the picture, aunt?"

"My child, you ask very queer questions. If your mamma don't like the picture, it is for a very plain reason. She has a much larger and finer one at home, which she had painted for herself; yes, and paid I don't know how many hundred dollars for it; and that, too, is an excellent likeness, *that* must be the reason, little Pierre."

And thus the old aunt and the little child ran on; each thinking the other very strange; and both thinking the picture still stranger; and the face in the picture still looked at them frankly, and cheerfully, as if there was nothing kept concealed; and yet again, a little ambiguously and mockingly, as if slyly winking to some other picture, to mark what a very foolish old sister, and what a very silly little son, were growing so monstrously grave and speculative about a huge white-figured neckcloth, a buff vest, and a very gentleman-like and amiable countenance.

And so, after this scene, as usual, one by one, the fleet years ran on; till the little child Pierre had grown up to be the tall Master Pierre, and could call the picture his own; and now, in the privacy of his own little closet, could stand, or lean, or sit before it all day long, if he pleased, and keep thinking, and thinking, and thinking, and thinking, till by-and-by all thoughts were blurred, and at last there were no thoughts at all.

Before the picture was sent to him, in his fifteenth year, it had been only through the inadvertence of his mother, or rather through a casual passing into a parlor by Pierre, that he had any way learned that his mother did not approve of the picture. Because, as then Pierre was still young, and the picture was the picture of his father, and the cherished property of a most excellent, and dearly-beloved, affectionate aunt; therefore the mother, with an intuitive delicacy, had refrained from knowingly expressing her peculiar opinion in the presence of little Pierre. And this judicious, though half-unconscious delicacy in the mother, had been perhaps somewhat singularly answered by a like nicety of sentiment in the child; for children of a naturally refined organization, and a gentle nurture, sometimes possess a wonderful, and often undreamed-of daintiness of propriety, and thoughtfulness, and forbearance, in matters esteemed a little subtile even by their elders, and self-elected betters. The little Pierre never disclosed to his mother that he had, through another person, become aware of her thoughts concerning Aunt Dorothea's portrait; he seemed to possess an intuitive knowledge of the circumstance, that from the difference of their relationship to his father, and for other minute reasons, he could in some things, with the greater propriety, be more inquisitive concerning him, with his aunt, than with his mother, especially touching the matter of the chair-portrait. And Aunt Dorothea's reasons accounting for his mother's distaste, long continued satisfactory, or at least not unsufficiently explanatory.

And when the portrait arrived at the Meadows, it so chanced that his mother was abroad; and so Pierre silently hung it up in his closet; and when after a day or two his mother returned, he said nothing to her about its arrival, being still strangely alive to that certain mild mystery which invested it, and whose sacredness now he was fearful of violating, by provoking any discussion with his mother about Aunt Dorothea's gift, or by permitting himself to be improperly curious concerning the reasons of his mother's private and self-reserved opinions of it. But the first time—and it was not long after the arrival of the portrait—that he knew of his mother's having entered his closet; then, when he next saw her, he was prepared to hear what she should voluntarily say about the late addition to its embellishments; but as she omitted all mention of any thing of that sort, he unobtrusively scanned her countenance, to mark whether any little clouding emotion might be discoverable there. But he could discern none. And as all genuine delicacies are by their nature accumulative; therefore this reverential, mutual, but only tacit forbearance of the mother and son, ever after continued uninvaded. And it was another sweet, and sanctified, and sanctifying bond between them. For, whatever some lovers may sometimes say, love does not always abhor a secret, as nature is said to abhor a vacuum.

Love is built upon secrets, as lovely Venice upon invisible and incorruptible piles in the sea. Love's secrets, being mysteries, ever pertain to the transcendent and the infinite; and so they are as airy bridges, by which our further shadows pass over into the regions of the golden mists and exhalations; whence all poetical, lovely thoughts are engendered, and drop into us, as though pearls should drop from rainbows.

As time went on, the chasteness and pure virginity of this mutual reservation, only served to dress the portrait in sweeter, because still more mysterious attractions; and to fling, as it were, fresh fennel and rosemary around the revered memory of the father. Though, indeed, as previously recounted, Pierre now and then loved to present to himself for some fanciful solution the penultimate secret of the portrait, in so far as that involved his mother's distaste; yet the cunning analysis in which such a mental procedure would involve him, never voluntarily transgressed that sacred limit, where his mother's peculiar repugnance began to shade off into ambiguous considerations, touching any unknown possibilities in the character and early life of the original. Not, that he had altogether forbidden his fancy to range in such fields of speculation; but all such imaginings must be contributory to that pure, exalted idea of his father, which, in his soul, was based upon the known acknowledged facts of his father's life.

If, when the mind roams up and down in the ever-elastic regions of evanescent invention, any definite form or feature can be assigned to the multitudinous shapes it creates out of the incessant dissolvings of its own prior creations; then might we here attempt to hold and define the least shadowy of those reasons, which about the period of adolescence we now treat of, more frequently occurred to Pierre, whenever he essayed to account for his mother's remarkable distaste for the portrait. Yet will we venture one sketch.

Yes—sometimes dimly thought Pierre—who knows but cousin Ralph, after all, may have been not so very far from the truth, when he surmised that at one time my father did indeed cherish some passing emotion for the beautiful young Frenchwoman. And this portrait being painted at that precise time, and indeed with the precise purpose of perpetuating some shadowy testification of the fact in the countenance of the original: therefore, its expression is not congenial, is not familiar, is not altogether agreeable to my mother: because, not only did my father's features never look so to her (since it was afterward that she first became acquainted with him), but also, that certain womanliness of women; that thing I should perhaps call a tender jealousy, a fastidious vanity, in any other lady, enables her to perceive that the glance of the face in the portrait, is not, in some nameless way, dedicated to herself, but to some other and unknown object; and therefore, is she impatient of it, and it is repelling to her; for she must naturally be intolerant of any imputed reminiscence in my father, which is not in some way connected with her own recollections of him.

Whereas, the larger and more expansive portrait in the great drawing-room, taken in the prime of life; during the best and rosiest days of their wedded union; at the particular desire of my mother; and by a celebrated artist of her own election, and costumed after her own taste; and on all hands considered to be, by those who know, a singularly happy likeness at the period; a belief spiritually reinforced by my own dim infantile remembrances; for all these reasons, this drawing-room portrait possesses an inestimable charm to her; there, she indeed beholds her husband as he had really appeared to her; she does not vacantly gaze upon an unfamiliar phantom called up from the distant, and, to her, well-nigh fabulous days of my father's bachelor life. But in that other portrait, she sees rehearsed to her fond eyes, the latter tales and legends of his devoted wedded love. Yes, I think now that I plainly see it must be so. And yet, ever new conceits come vaporing up in me, as I look on the strange chair-portrait: which, though so very much more unfamiliar to me, than it can possibly be to my mother, still sometimes seems to say—Pierre, believe not the drawing-room painting; that is not thy father; or, at least, is not *all* of thy father. Consider in thy mind, Pierre, whether we two paintings may not make only one. Faithful wives are ever over-fond to a certain imaginary image of their husbands; and faithful widows are ever over-reverential to a certain imagined ghost of that same imagined image, Pierre. Look, again, I am thy father as he more truly was. In mature life, the world overlays and varnishes us, Pierre; the thousand proprieties and polished finenesses and grimaces intervene, Pierre; then, we, as it were, abdicate ourselves, and take unto us another self, Pierre; in youth we *are*, Pierre, but in age we *seem*. Look again. I am thy real father, so much the more truly, as thou thinkest thou recognizest me not, Pierre. To their young children, fathers are not wont to unfold themselves entirely, Pierre. There are a thousand and one odd little youthful peccadilloes, that we think we may as well not divulge to them, Pierre. Consider this strange, ambiguous smile, Pierre; more narrowly regard this mouth. Behold, what is this too ardent and, as it were, unchastened light in these eyes, Pierre? I am thy father, boy. There was once a certain, oh, but too lovely young

Frenchwoman, Pierre. Youth is hot, and temptation strong, Pierre; and in the minutest moment momentous things are irrevocably done, Pierre; and Time sweeps on, and the thing is not always carried down by its stream, but may be left stranded on its bank; away beyond, in the young, green countries, Pierre. Look again. Doth thy mother dislike me for naught? Consider. Do not all her spontaneous, loving impressions, ever strive to magnify, and spiritualize, and deify, her husband's memory, Pierre? Then why doth she cast despite upon me; and never speak to thee of me; and why dost thou thyself keep silence before her, Pierre? Consider. Is there no little mystery here? Probe a little, Pierre. Never fear, never fear. No matter for thy father now. Look, do I not smile?— yes, and with an unchangeable smile; and thus have I unchangeably smiled for many long years gone by, Pierre. Oh, it is a permanent smile! Thus I smiled to cousin Ralph; and thus in thy dear old Aunt Dorothea's parlor, Pierre; and just so, I smile here to thee, and even thus in thy father's later life, when his body may have been in grief, still—hidden away in Aunt Dorothea's secretary—I thus smiled as before; and just so I'd smile were I now hung up in the deepest dungeon of the Spanish Inquisition, Pierre; though suspended in outer darkness, still would I smile with this smile, though then not a soul should be near. Consider; for a smile is the chosen vehicle of all ambiguities, Pierre. When we would deceive, we smile; when we are hatching any nice little artifice, Pierre; only just a little gratifying our own sweet little appetites, Pierre; then watch us, and out comes the odd little smile. Once upon a time, there was a lovely young Frenchwoman, Pierre. Have you carefully, and analytically, and psychologically, and metaphysically, considered her belongings and surroundings, and all her incidentals, Pierre? Oh, a strange sort of story, that, thy dear old Aunt Dorothea once told thee, Pierre. I once knew a credulous old soul, Pierre. Probe, probe a little—see—there seems one little crack there, Pierre—a wedge, a wedge. Something ever comes of all persistent inquiry; we are not so continually curious for nothing, Pierre; not for nothing, do we so intrigue and become wily diplomatists, and glozers with our own minds, Pierre; and afraid of following the Indian trail from the open plain into the dark thickets, Pierre; but enough; a word to the wise.

Thus sometimes in the mystical, outer quietude of the long country nights; either when the hushed mansion was banked round by the thickfallen December snows, or banked round by the immovable white August moonlight; in the haunted repose of a wide story, tenanted only by himself; and sentineling his own little closet; and standing guard, as it were, before the mystical tent of the picture; and ever watching the strangely concealed lights of the meanings that so mysteriously moved to and fro within; thus sometimes stood Pierre before the portrait of his father, unconsciously throwing himself open to all those ineffable hints and ambiguities, and undefined half-suggestions, which now and then people the soul's atmosphere, as thickly as in a soft, steady snow-storm, the snow-flakes people the air. Yet as often starting from these reveries and trances, Pierre would regain the assured element of consciously bidden and self-propelled thought; and then in a moment the air all cleared, not a snow-flake descended, and Pierre, upbraiding himself for his self-indulgent infatuation, would promise never again to fall into a midnight revery before the chair-portrait of his father. Nor did the streams of these reveries seem to leave any conscious sediment in his mind; they were so light and so rapid, that they rolled their own alluvial along; and seemed to leave all Pierre's thought-channels as clean and dry as though never any alluvial stream had rolled there at all.

And so still in his sober, cherishing memories, his father's beatification remained untouched; and all the strangeness of the portrait only served to invest his idea with a fine, legendary romance; the essence whereof was that very mystery, which at other times was so subtly and evilly significant.

But now, *now!*—Isabel's letter read; swift as the first light that slides from the sun, Pierre saw all preceding ambiguities, all mysteries ripped open as if with a keen sword, and forth trooped thickening phantoms of an infinite gloom. Now his remotest infantile reminiscences—the wandering mind of his father—the empty hand, and the ashen—the strange story of Aunt Dorothea—the mystical midnight suggestions of the portrait itself; and, above all, his mother's intuitive aversion, all, all overwhelmed him with reciprocal testimonies.

And now, by irresistible intuitions, all that had been inexplicably mysterious to him in the portrait, and all that had been inexplicably familiar in the face, most magically these now coincided; the merriness of the one not inharmonious with the mournfulness of the other, but by some ineffable correlativeness, they reciprocally identified each other, and, as it were, melted into each other, and thus interpenetratingly uniting, presented lineaments of an added supernaturalness.

On all sides, the physical world of solid objects now slidingly displaced itself from around him, and he floated into an ether of visions; and, starting to his feet with clenched hands and outstaring eyes at the transfixed face in the air, he ejaculated that wonderful verse from Dante, descriptive of the two mutually absorbing shapes in the Inferno:

"Ah! how dost thou change, Agnello! See! thou art not double now,
Nor only one!"

It was long after midnight when Pierre returned to the house. He had
rushed forth in that complete abandonment of soul, which, in so ardent a
temperament, attends the first stages of any sudden and tremendous afflic-
tion; but now he returned in pallid composure, for the calm spirit of the
night, and the then risen moon, and the late revealed stars, had all at last
become as a strange subduing melody to him, which, though at first trampled
and scorned, yet by degrees had stolen into the windings of his heart, and
so shed abroad its own quietude in him. Now, from his height of composure, he firmly gazed abroad upon the charred landscape within him; as the
timber man of Canada, forced to fly from the conflagration of his forests,
comes back again when the fires have waned, and unblinkingly eyes the
immeasurable fields of fire-brands that here and there glow beneath the
wide canopy of smoke.

It has been said, that always when Pierre would seek solitude in its
material shelter and walled isolation, then the closet communicating with
his chamber was his elected haunt. So, going to his room, he took up the
now dim-burning lamp he had left there, and instinctively entered that retreat, seating himself, with folded arms and bowed head, in the accustomed
dragon-footed old chair. With leaden feet, and heart now changing from
iciness to a strange sort of indifference, and a numbing sensation stealing
over him, he sat there awhile, till, like the resting traveler in snows, he began
to struggle against this inertness as the most treacherous and deadliest of
symptoms. He looked up, and found himself fronted by the no longer wholly
enigmatical, but still ambiguously smiling picture of his father. Instantly all
his consciousness and his anguish returned, but still without power to shake
the grim tranquillity which possessed him. Yet endure the smiling portrait
he could not; and obeying an irresistible nameless impulse, he rose, and
without unhanging it, reversed the picture on the wall.

This brought to sight the defaced and dusty back, with some wrinkled,
tattered paper over the joints, which had become loosened from the paste.
"Oh, symbol of thy reversed idea in my soul," groaned Pierre; "thou shalt
not hang thus. Rather cast thee utterly out, than conspicuously insult thee
so. I will no more have a father." He removed the picture wholly from the
wall, and the closet; and concealed it in a large chest, covered with blue
chintz, and locked it up there. But still, in a square space of slightly discol-

ored wall, the picture still left its shadowy, but vacant and desolate trace. He now strove to banish the least trace of his altered father, as fearful that at present all thoughts concerning him were not only entirely vain, but would prove fatally distracting and incapacitating to a mind, which was now loudly called upon, not only to endure a signal grief, but immediately to act upon it. Wild and cruel case, youth ever thinks; but mistakenly; for Experience well knows, that action, though it seems an aggravation of woe, is really an alleviative; though permanently to alleviate pain, we must first dart some added pangs.

Pricking and Polishing Your Bright-Work

This excerpt from White-Jacket *discusses how sailors kill time on a ship. Again, Melville is in* double entendre *mode in this excerpt.*

This excerpt contains chapter 42 of the novel. The title is the editor's based on Melville's text, but is not his title for the chapter.

Reading was by no means the only method adopted by my shipmates in whiling away the long, tedious hours in harbour. In truth, many of them could not have read, had they wanted to ever so much; in their early youth their primers had been sadly neglected. Still, they had other pursuits; some were expert at the needle, and employed their time in making elaborate shirts, stitching picturesque eagles, and anchors, and all the stars of the federated states in the collars thereof; so that when they at last completed and put on these shirts, they may be said to have hoisted the American colours.

Others excelled in *tattooing*, or *pricking*, as it is called in a man-of-war. Of these prickers, two had long been celebrated, in their way, as consumate masters of the art. Each had a small box full of tools and colouring matter; and they charged so high for their services, that at the end of the cruise they were supposed to have cleared upward of four hundred dollars. They would *prick* you to order a palm-tree, an anchor, a crucifix, a lady, a lion, an eagle, or anything else you might want.

The Roman Catholic sailors on board had at least the crucifix pricked on their arms, and for this reason: if they chanced to die in a Catholic land, they would be sure of a decent burial in consecrated ground, as the priest would be sure to observe the symbol of Mother Church on their persons. They would not fare as Protestant sailors dying in Callao, who are shoved under the sands of St. Lorenzo, a solitary, volcanic island in the harbour, overrun with reptiles, their heretical bodies not being permitted to repose in the more genial loam of Lima.

And many sailors not Catholics were anxious to have the crucifix painted on them, owing to a curious superstition of their. They affirm—some of them—that if you have thatmark tatooed upon all four limbs, you might fall overboard among seven hundred and seventy five thousand white sharks, all dinnerless, and not one of them would do so much as dare to smell at your little finger.

We had one foretop-man on board, who, during the entire cruise, was having an endless cable *pricked* round and round his waist, so that, when his frock was off, he looked like a capstan with a hawser coiled round about it. This foretop-man paid eighteen pence per link for the cable, besides being on the smart the whole cruise, suffering the effects of his repeated puncturings; so he paid very dear for his cable.

One other mode of passing time while in port was cleaning and polishing your *bright-work*; for it must be known that, in men-of-war, every sailor has some brass or steel of one kind or another to keep in high order—like housemaids, whose business it is to keep well polished the knobs on the front-door railing and the parlour grates.

Excepting the ring-bolts, eye-bolts, and belaying-pins scattered about the decks, this bright-work, as it is called, is principally about the guns embracing the *monkey-tails* of the carronades, the screws, *prickers*, little irons, and other things.

The portion that fell to my own share I kept in superior order, quite equal in polish to Roger's best cutlery. I received the most extravagant encomiums from the officers; one of whom offered to match me against any brasier or brass-polisher in Her British Majesty's Navy. Indeed, I devoted myself to the work body and soul, and thought no pains too painful, and no labour too laborious, to acheive the highest attainable polish possible for us poor lost sons of Adam to reach.

Upon one occasion, even, when woollen rags were scarce, and no burned-brick was to be had from the ship's yeoman, I sacrificed the corners of my woolen shirt, and used some dentifrice I had, as substitutes for the rags and burned-brick. The dentifrice operated delightfully, and made the threading of my carronade-screw shine and grin again, like a set of false teeth in an eager heiress-hunter's mouth.

Still another mode of passing time, was arraying yourself in your best *togs*, and promenading up and down the gun-deck, admiring the shore scenery from the port-holes, which, in an amphitheatrical bay like Rio—belted about by the most varied and charming scenery of hill, dale, moss, meadow, court, castle, tower, groove, vine, vineyard, aqueduct, palace, square, island, fort—is very much like lounging round a circular cosmorama, and ever and anon lazily peeping through the glasses here and there. Oh! there is something worth living for, even in our man-of-war world; and one glimpse of a bower of grapes through a cable's length off, is almost satisfaction for dining off a shank-bone salted down.

This promenading was chiefly patronized by the marines, and particularly by Colbrook, a remarkably handsome and very gentlemanly corporal among them. He was a complete lady's man; with fine eyes, bright red cheeks, glossy jet whiskers, and a refined organization of the whole man. He used to array himself in his regiments, and saunter about like an officer of the Coldstream Guards, strolling down to his club in St. James's. Every time he passed me he would heave a sentimental sigh, and hum to himself *The Girl I left behind me.* This fine corporal aferward became a representative in the legislature of the state of New Jersey; for I saw his name returned about a year after my return home.

But, after all, there was not much room, while in port, for promenading, at least on the gun deck, for the whole larboard side is kept clear for the benefit of the officers, who appreciate the advantages of having a clear stroll fore and aft; and well they know that the sailors had much better be crowded together on the other side than that the set of their own coat-tails should be impaired by brushing against their tarry trowsers.

One other way of killing time while in port is playing checkers; that is, when it is permitted; for it is not every Navy captain who will allow such a scandalous proceeding. But, as for Captain Claret, though he *did* like his glass of Madeira uncommonly well, and was an undoubted descendant from the hero of the Battle of the Brandywine, and though he sometimes showed a suspiciously flushed face when superintending in person the flogging of a sailor for getting intoxicated against his particular orders, yet I will say for Captain Claret that, upon the whole, he was rather indulgent to his crew, so long as they were perfectly docile. He allowed them to play checkers as much as they pleased. More than once have I known him, when going forward to the forecastle, pick his way carfully among scores of canvass checker-cloths spread upon the deck, so as not to tread upon the men—the checker-men and the man-of-war's-men included; but, in a certain state, they were both one; for, as the sailors used their checker-men, so, at quarters, their officers used these man-of-war's-men.

But Captain Claret's leniency in permitting checkers on board his ship might have arisen from the following little circumstance, confidentially communicated to me. Soon after the ship had sailed from home, checkers were prohibited; whereupon the sailors were exasperated against the captain, and one night, when he was walking round the forecastle, bim! came an iron belaying-pin past his ears; and while he was dodging that, bim! came another, from the other side so that, it being a very dark night, and nobody to be seen, and it being impossible to find out the trespassers, he thought it best to get back into his cabin as soon as possible. Some time after—just as if the belaying-pins had nothing to do with it—it was indirectly rumoured that the checker-boards might be brought out again, which—as a philosophical shipmate observed—showed that Captain Claret was a man of ready understanding, and could understand a hint as well as any other man, even when conveyed by several pounds of iron.

Some of the sailors were very precise about their checker-cloths, and even went so far that they would not let you play with them unless you first washed your hands, especially if so be you had just come from tarring down the rigging.

Another way of beguiling the tedious hours, is to get a cosy seat somewhere, and fall into as snug a little reverie as you can. Or if a seat is not to be had—which is frequently the case—then get a tolerably comfortable *stand-up* against the bulwarks, and begin to think about home and bread and butter—always inseparably connected to a wanderer—which will very soon bring delicious tears into your eyes; for every one knows what a luxury is grief, when you can get a private closet to enjoy it in, and no Paul Prys intrude. Several of my shore friends, indeed, when suddenly overwhelmed by some disaster, always make a point of flying to the first oyster-cellar, and shutting themselves up in a box, with nothing but a plate of stewed oysters, some crackers, the castor, and a decanter of port.

Still another way of killing time in harbour, is to lean over the bulwarks, and speculate upon where under the sun you are going to be that day next year, which is a subject full of interest to every living soul; so much so, that there is a particular day of a particular month of the year, which, from my earliest recollections, I have always kept run of, so that I can even now tell just where I was on that identical day of every year past since I was twelve years old. And when I am all alone, to run over this almanac in my mind is almost as entertaining as to read my diary, and far more interesting than to persue a table of alogrithms on a rainy afternoon. I always keep the anniversary of that day with lamb and peas, and a pint of sherry, for it comes in spring. But when it came round in the *Neversink*, I could get neither lamb, peas, nor sherry.

But perhaps the best way to drive the hours before you four-in-hand, is to select a soft plank on the gun deck, and go to sleep. A fine specific, which seldom fails, unless, to be sure, you have been sleeping all the twenty-four hours beforehand.

Whenever employed in killing time in harbour, I have lifted myself up on my elbow and looked around me, and seen so many of my shipmates all employed at the same common business; all under lock and key; all hopeless prisoners like myself; all under martial law; all dieting on salt beef and biscuit; all in one uniform; all yawning, gaping, and stretching in concert, it was then I used to feel a certain love and affection for them, grounded, doubtless, on a fellow-feeling.

And though, in a previous part of this narrative, I have mentioned that I used to hold myself somewhat aloof from the mass of seamen on board the *Neversink*; and though this was true, and my real acquaintances were comparatively few, and my intimacies still fewer, yet, to tell the truth, it is quite impossible to live to long with five hundred of your fellow-beings, even if not of the best families in the land, and with morals that would not be spoiled by further cultivation; it is quite impossible, I say, to live with five hundred of your fellow-beings, be they who they may, without a feeling a common sympathy with them at the time, and ever after cherishing some sort of interest in their welfare.

Billy Budd, Sailor

Billy Budd is perhaps the motherlode for gay readers of Melville. We have, perhaps for the first time in literature, a detailed examination of the results of internalized homophobia. While the sailor Billy is admired by all for his physical beauty, Claggart, who longs for him but cannot possess him, brings him down.

A brief introduction such as this cannot hope to capture the gay significance of this major work; it is best left for readers to discover this for themselves. One detail to note: in chapter 26, the 'muscular spasm' referred to is the phenomenon of ejaculation occurring when the spinal cord is snapped. The characters in this chapter are struck by the absense of this.

1

In the time before steamships, or then more frequently than now, a stroller along the docks of any considerable sea-port would occasionally have his attention arrested by a group of bronzed mariners, man-of-war's men or me chant-sailors in holiday attire, ashore on liberty. In certain instances they would flank, or like a body-guard quite surround, some superior figure of their own class, moving along with them like Aldebaran among the lesser lights of his constellation. That signal object was the "Handsome Sailor" of the less prosaic time alike of the military and merchant navies. With no perceptible trace of the vain-glorious about him, rather with the off-hand unaffectedness of natural regality, he seemed to accept the spontaneous homage of his shipmates.

A somewhat remarkable instance recurs to me. In Liverpool, now half a century ago, I saw under the shadow of the great dingy street-wall of Prince's Dock (an obstruction long since removed) a common sailor so intensely black that he must needs have been a native African of the unadulterate blood of Ham—a symmetric figure much above the average height. The two ends of a gay silk handkerchief thrown loose about the neck danced upon the displayed ebony of his chest, in his ears were big hoops of gold, and a Scotch Highland bonnet with a tartan band set off his shapely head. It was a hot noon in July; and his face, lustrous with perspiration, beamed with barbaric good humor. In jovial sallies right and left, his white teeth flashing into view he rollicked along, the center of a company of his shipmates. These were made up of such an assortment of tribes and complexions as would have well fitted them to be marched up by Anacharsis Cloots before the bar of the first French Assembly as Representatives of the Human Race. At each spontaneous tribute rendered by the wayfarers to this black pagod of a fellow—the tribute of a pause and stare, and less frequent an exclamation—the motley retinue showed that they took that sort of pride in the evoker of it which the Assyrian priests doubtless showed for their grand sculptured Bull when the faithful prostrated themselves.

To return. If in some cases a bit of a nautical Murat in setting forth his person ashore, the Handsome Sailor of the period in question evinced nothing of the dandified Billy-be-Dam, an amusing character all but extinct now, but occasionally to be encountered, and in a form yet more amusing than the original, at the tiller of the boats on the tempestuous Erie Canal or, more likely, vaporing in the groggeries along the towpath. Invariably a proficient in his perilous calling, he was also more or less of a mighty boxer or wrestler. It was strength and beauty. Tales of his prowess were recited. Ashore he was the champion; afloat the spokesman; on every suitable occasion always foremost. Close-reefing topsails in a gale, there he was, astride the weather yardarm-end, foot in the Flemish horse as stirrup, both hands tugging at the earring as at a bridle, in very much the attitude of young Alexander curbing the fiery Bucephalus. A superb figure, tossed up as by the horns of Taurus against the thunderous sky, cheerily hallooing to the strenuous file along the spar.

The moral nature was seldom out of keeping with the physical make. Indeed, except as toned by the former, the comeliness and power, always attractive in masculine conjunction, hardly could have drawn the sort of honest homage the Handsome Sailor in some examples received from his less gifted associates.

Such a cynosure, at least in aspect, and something such too in nature, though with important variations made apparent as the story proceeds, was welkin-eyed Billy Budd—or Baby Budd, as more familiarly under circumstances hereafter to be given, he at last came to be called—aged twenty-one, a foretopman of the British fleet toward the close of the last decade of the eighteenth century. It was not very long prior to the time of the narration that follows that he had entered the King's Service, having been impressed on the Narrow Seas from a homeward-bound English merchantman into a seventy-four outward bound, H.M.S. *Bellipotent*; which ship, as was not unusual in those hurried days, having been obliged to put to sea short of her proper complement of men. Plump upon Billy at first sight in the gangway the boarding officer, Lieutenant Ratcliff, pounced, even before the merchantman's crew was formally mustered on the quarter-deck for his deliberate inspection. And him only he elected. For whether it was because the other men when ranged before him showed to ill advantage after Billy, or whether he had some scruples in view of the merchantman's being rather shorthanded, however it might be, the officer contented himself with his first spontaneous choice. To the surprise of the ship's company, though much to the lieutenant's satisfaction, Billy made no demur. But, indeed, any demur would have been as idle as the protest of a goldfinch popped into a cage.

Noting this uncomplaining acquiescence, all but cheerful, one might say, the shipmates turned a surprised glance of silent reproach at the sailor. The shipmaster was one of those worthy mortals found in every vocation, even the humbler ones—the sort of person whom everybody agrees in calling "a respectable man." And—nor so strange to report as it may appear to be—though a ploughman of the troubled waters, life-long contending with the intractable elements, there was nothing this honest soul at heart loved better than simple peace and quiet. For the rest, he was fifty or thereabouts, a little inclined to corpulence, a prepossessing face, unwhiskered, and of an agreeable color—a rather full face, humanely intelligent in expression. On a fair day with a fair wind and all going well, a certain musical chime in his voice seemed to be the veritable unobstructed outcome of the innermost man. He had much prudence, much conscientiousness, and there were occasions when these virtues were the cause of overmuch disquietude in him. On a passage, so long as his craft was in any proximity to land, no sleep for Captain Graveling. He took to heart those serious responsibilities not so heavily borne by some shipmasters.

Now while Billy Budd was down in the forecastle getting his kit together, the *Bellipotent's* Lieutenant, burly and bluff, nowise disconcerted by Captain Graveling's omitting to proffer the customary hospitalities on an occasion so unwelcome to him, an omission simply caused by preoccupation of thought, unceremoniously invited himself into the cabin, and also to a flask from the spirit locker, a receptacle which his experienced eye instantly discovered. In fact he was one of those sea dogs in whom all the hardship and peril of naval life in the great prolonged wars of his time never impaired the natural instinct for sensuous enjoyment. His duty he always faithfully did; but duty is sometimes a dry obligation, and he was for irrigating its aridity, whensoever possible, with a fertilizing decoction of strong waters. For the cabin's proprietor there was nothing left but to play the part of the enforced host with whatever grace and alacrity were practicable. As necessary adjuncts to the flask, he silently placed tumbler and water jug before the irrepressible guest. But excusing himself from partaking just then, he dismally watched the unembarrassed officer deliberately diluting his grog a little, then tossing it off in three swallows, pushing the empty tumbler away, yet not so far as to be beyond easy reach, at the same time settling himself in his seat and smacking his lips with high satisfaction, looking straight at the host.

These proceedings over, the master broke the silence; and there lurked a rueful reproach in the tone of his voice: "Lieutenant, you are going to take my best man from me, the jewel of 'em."

"Yes, I know," rejoined the other, immediately drawing back the tumbler preliminary to a replenishing. "Yes, I know. Sorry."

"Beg pardon, but you don't understand, Lieutenant. See here, now. Before I shipped that young fellow, my forecastle was a rat-pit of quarrels. It was black times, I tell you, aboard the *Rights* here. I was worried to that degree my pipe had no comfort for me. But Billy came; and it was like a Catholic priest striking peace in an Irish shindy. Not that he preached to them or said or did anything in particular; but a virtue went out of him, sugaring the sour ones. They took to him like hornets to treacle; all but the buffer of the gang, the big shaggy chap with the fire-red whiskers. He indeed, out of envy, perhaps, of the newcomer, and thinking such a 'sweet and pleasant fellow,' as he mockingly designated him to the others, could hardly have the spirit of a gamecock, must needs bestir himself in trying to get up an ugly row with him. Billy forebore with him and reasoned with him in a pleasant way—he is something like myself, Lieutenant, to whom aught like a quarrel is hateful—but nothing served. So, in the second dog-watch one day the Red Whiskers in presence of the others, under pretense of showing Billy just whence a sirloin steak was cut—for the fellow had once been a butcher—insultingly gave him a dig under the ribs. Quick as lightning Billy let fly his arm. I dare say he never meant to do quite as much as he did, but anyhow he gave the burly fool a terrible drubbing. It took about half a minute, I should think. And, lord bless you, the lubber was astonished at the celerity. And will you believe it, Lieutenant, the Red Whiskers now really loves Billy—loves him, or is the biggest hypocrite that ever I heard of. But they all love him. Some of 'em do his washing, darn his old trousers for him; the carpenter is at odd times making a pretty little chest of drawers for him. Anybody will do anything for Billy Budd; and it's the happy family here. But now, Lieutenant, if that young fellow goes—I know how it will be aboard the *Rights*. Not again very soon shall I, coming up from dinner, lean over the capstan smoking a quiet pipe—no, not very soon again, I think. Ay, Lieutenant, you are going to take away the jewel of 'em; you are going to take away my peacemaker!" And with that the good soul had really some ado in checking a rising sob.

"Well," said the officer who had listened with amused interest to all this and now waxing merry with his tipple; "well, blessed are the peacemakers, especially the fighting peacemakers. And such are the seventy-four beauties some of which you see poking their noses out of the port-holes of yonder warship lying to for me," pointing through the cabin window at the *Bellipotent*. "But courage! Don't look so downhearted, man. Why, I pledge you in advance the royal approbation. Rest assured that His Majesty will be delighted to know that in a time when his hardtack is not sought for by sailors with such avidity as should be, a time also when some shipmasters privily resent the borrowing from them a tar or two for the service; His Majesty, I say, will be delighted to learn that *one* shipmaster at least cheerfully surrenders to the King the flower of his flock, a sailor who with equal loyalty makes no dissent.—But where's my beauty? Ah," looking through the cabin's open door, "here he comes; and, by Jove, lugging along his chest—Apollo with his portmanteau!—My man," stepping out to him, "you can't take that big box aboard a war-ship. The boxes there are mostly shot boxes. Put your duds in a bag, lad. Boot and saddle for the cavalryman, bag and hammock for the man-of-war's man."

The transfer from chest to bag was made. And, after seeing his man into the cutter and then following him down, the Lieutenant pushed off from the *Rights-of-Man*. That was the merchant ship's name; though by her master and crew abbreviated in sailor fashion into the *Rights*. The hardheaded Dundee owner was a staunch admirer of Thomas Paine, whose book in rejoinder to Burke's arraignment of the French Revolution had then been published for some time and had gone everywhere. In christening his vessel after the title of Paine's volume the man of Dundee was something like his contemporary shipowner, Stephen Girard of Philadelphia, whose sympathies, alike with his native land and its liberal philosophers, he evinced by naming his ships after Voltaire, Diderot, and so forth.

But now, when the boat swept under the merchantman's stern, and officer and oarsmen were noting—some bitterly and others with a grin—the name emblazoned there; just then it was that the new recruit jumped up from the bow where the coxswain had directed him to sit, and waving his hat to his silent shipmates sorrowfully looking over at him from the taffrail, bade the lads a genial good-bye. Then, making a salutation as to the ship herself, "And good-bye to you too, old *Rights-of-Man.*"

"Down, Sir!" roared the Lieutenant, instantly assuming all the rigor of his rank, though with difficulty repressing a smile.

To be sure, Billy's action was a terrible breach of naval decorum. But in that decorum he had never been instructed; in consideration of which the Lieutenant would hardly have been so energetic in reproof but for the concluding farewell to the ship. This he rather took as meant to convey a covert sally on the new recruit's part, a sly slur at impressment in general, and that of himself in especial. And yet, more likely, if satire it was in effect, it was hardly so by intention, for Billy, though happily endowed with the gayety of high health, youth, and a free heart, was yet by no means of a satirical turn. The will to it and the sinister dexterity were alike wanting. To deal in double meanings and insinuations of any sort was quite foreign to his nature.

As to his enforced enlistment, that he seemed to take pretty much as he was wont to take any vicissitude of weather. Like the animals, though no philosopher, he was, without knowing it, practically a fatalist. And it may be that he rather liked this adventurous turn in his affairs, which promised an opening into novel scenes and martial excitements.

Aboard the *Bellipotent* our merchant sailor was forthwith rated as an able-seaman and assigned to the starboard watch of the foretop. He was soon at home in the service, not at all disliked for his unpretentious good looks and a sort of genial happy-go-lucky air. No merrier man in his mess: in marked contrast to certain other individuals included like himself among the impressed portion of the ship's company; for these when not actively employed were sometimes, and more particularly in the last dogwatch when the drawing near of twilight induced revery, apt to fall into a saddish mood which in some partook of sullenness. But they were not so young as our foretopman, and no few of them must have known a hearth of some sort, others may have had wives and children left, too probably, in uncertain circumstances, and hardly any but must have had acknowledged kith and kin, while for Billy, as will shortly be seen, his entire family was practically invested in himself.

2

Though our new-made foretopman was well received in the top and on the gun decks, hardly here was he that cynosure he had previously been among those minor ship's companies of the merchant marine, with which companies only had he hitherto consorted.

He was young; and despite his all but fully developed frame, in aspect looked even younger than he really was, owing to a lingering adolescent expression in the as yet smooth face all but feminine in purity of natural complexion but where, thanks to his seagoing, the lily was quite suppressed and the rose had some ado visibly to flush through the tan.

To one essentially such a novice in the complexities of factitious life, the abrupt transition from his former and simpler sphere to the ampler and more knowing world of a great warship; this might well have abashed him had there been any conceit or vanity in his composition. Among her miscellaneous multitude, the *Bellipotent* mustered several individuals who however inferior in grade were of no common natural stamp, sailors more signally susceptive of that air which continuous martial discipline and repeated presence in battle can in some degree impart even to the average man. As the Handsome Sailor, Billy Budd's position aboard the seventy-four was something analogous to that of a rustic beauty transplanted from the provinces and brought into competition with the highborn dames of the court. But this change of circumstances he scarce noted. As little did he observe that something about him provoked an ambiguous smile in one or two harder faces among the blue-jackets. Nor less unaware was he of the peculiar favorable effect his person and demeanour had upon the more intelligent gentlemen of the quarter-deck. Nor could this well have been otherwise. Cast in a mould peculiar to the finest physical examples of those Englishmen in whom the Saxon strain would seem not at all to partake of any Norman or other admixture, he showed in face that humane look of reposeful good nature which the Greek sculptor in some instances gave to his heroic strong man, Hercules. But this again was subtly modified by another and pervasive quality. The ear, small and shapely, the arch of the foot, the curve in mouth and nostril, even the indurated hand dyed to the orange-tawny of the toucan's bill, a hand telling alike of the halyards and tar bucket; but, above all, something in the mobile expression, and every chance attitude and movement, something suggestive of a mother eminently favored by Love and the Graces; all this strangely indicated a lineage in direct contradiction to his lot. The mysteriousness here became less mysterious through a matter of fact elicited when Billy at the capstan was being formally mustered into the service. Asked by the officer, a small brisk little gentleman as it chanced, among other questions, his place of birth, he replied, "Please, sir, I don't know."

"Don't know where you were born? Who was your father?"

"God knows, sir."

Struck by the straightforward simplicity of these replies, the officer next asked, "Do you know anything about your beginning?"

"No, Sir. But I have heard that I was found in a pretty silk-lined basket hanging one morning from the knocker of a good man's door in Bristol."

"*Found*, say you? Well," throwing back his head and looking up and down the new recruit; "well, it turns out to have been a pretty good find. Hope they'll find some more like you, my man; the fleet sadly needs them."

Yes, Billy Budd was a foundling, a presumable by-blow, and, evidently, no ignoble one. Noble descent was as evident in him as in a blood horse.

For the rest, with little or no sharpness of faculty or any trace of the wisdom of the serpent, nor yet quite a dove, he possessed that kind and degree of intelligence going along with the unconventional rectitude of a sound human creature, one to whom not yet has been proffered the questionable apple of knowledge. He was illiterate; he could not read, but he could sing, and like the illiterate nightingale was sometimes the composer of his own song.

Of self-consciousness he seemed to have little or none, or about as much as we may reasonably impute to a dog of Saint Bernard's breed.

Habitually living with the elements and knowing little more of the land than as a beach, or, rather, that portion of the terraqueous globe providentially set apart for dance-houses, doxies and tapsters, in short what sailors call a "fiddlers' green," his simple nature remained unsophisticated by those moral obliquities which are not in every case incompatible with that manufacturable thing known as respectability. But are sailors, frequenters of fiddlers' greens, without vices? No; but less often than with landsmen do their vices, so called, partake of crookedness of heart, seeming less to proceed from viciousness than exuberance of vitality after long constraint: frank manifestations in accordance with natural law. By his original constitution aided by the co-operating influences of his lot, Billy in many respects was little more than a sort of upright barbarian, much such perhaps as Adam presumably might have been ere the urbane Serpent wriggled himself into his company.

And here be it submitted that apparently going to corroborate the doctrine of man's Fall, a doctrine now popularly ignored, it is observable that where certain virtues pristine and unadulterate peculiarly characterize anybody in the external uniform of civilization, they will upon scrutiny seem not to be derived from custom or convention, but rather to be out of keeping with these, as if indeed exceptionally transmitted from a period prior to Cain's city and citified man. The character marked by such qualities has to an unvitiated taste an untampered-with flavor like that of berries, while the man thoroughly civilized, even in a fair specimen of the breed, has to the same moral palate a questionable smack as of a compounded wine. To any stray inheritor of these primitive qualities found, like Caspar Hauser, wandering dazed in any Christian capital of our time, the good-natured poet's famous invocation, near two thousand years ago, of the good rustic out of his latitude in the Rome of the Caesars, still appropriately holds:

> Honest and poor, faithful in word and thought,
> What has thee, Fabian, to the city brought?

Though our Handsome Sailor had as much of masculine beauty as one can expect anywhere to see; nevertheless, like the beautiful woman in one of Hawthorne's minor tales, there was just one thing amiss in him. No visible blemish indeed, as with the lady; no, but an occasional liability to a vocal defect. Though in the hour of elemental uproar or peril he was everything that a sailor should be, yet under sudden provocation of strong heart-feeling his voice, otherwise singularly musical, as if expressive of the harmony within, was apt to develop an organic hesitancy, in fact more or less of a stutter or even worse. In this particular Billy was a striking instance that the arch interferer, the envious marplot of Eden, still has more or less to do with every human consignment to this planet of Earth. In every case, one way or another he is sure to slip in his little card, as much as to remind us—I too have a hand here.

The avowal of such an imperfection in the Handsome Sailor should be evidence not alone that he is not presented as a conventional hero, but also that the story in which he is the main figure is no romance.

3

At the time of Billy Budd's arbitrary enlistment into the *Bellipotent* that ship was on her way to join the Mediterranean fleet. No long time elapsed before the junction was effected. As one of that fleet the seventy-four participated in its movements, though at times on account of her superior sailing qualities, in the absence of frigates, dispatched on separate duty as a scout and at times on less temporary service. But with all this the story has little concernment, restricted as it is to the inner life of one particular ship and the career of an individual sailor.

It was the summer of 1797. In the April of that year had occurred the commotion at Spithead followed in May by a second and yet more serious outbreak in the fleet at the Nore. The latter is known, and without exaggeration in the epithet, as "the Great Mutiny." It was indeed a demonstration more menacing to England than the contemporary manifestoes and conquering and proselyting armies of the French Directory. To the British Empire the Nore Mutiny was what a strike in the fire-brigade would be to London threatened by general arson. In a crisis when the kingdom might well have anticipated the famous signal that some years later published along the naval line of battle what it was that upon occasion England expected of Englishmen; *that* was the time when at the mastheads of the three-deckers and seventy-fours moored in her own roadstead—a fleet the right arm of a Power then all but the sole free conservative one of the Old World—the bluejackets, to be numbered by thousands, ran up with huzzas the British colors with the union and cross wiped out; by that cancellation transmuting the flag of founded law and freedom defined, into the enemy's red meteor of unbridled and unbounded revolt. Reasonable discontent growing out of practical grievances in the fleet had been ignited into irrational combustion as by live cinders blown across the Channel from France in flames.

The event converted into irony for a time those spirited strains of Dibdin—as a song-writer no mean auxiliary to the English Government at the European conjuncture—strains celebrating, among other things, the patriotic devotion of the British tar: "And as for my life, 'tis the King's!"

Such an episode in the Island's grand naval story her naval historians naturally abridge; one of them (William James) candidly acknowledging that fain would he pass it over did not "impartiality forbid fastidiousness." And yet his mention is less a narration than a reference, having to do hardly at all with details. Nor are these readily to be found in the libraries. Like some other events in every age befalling states everywhere, including America, the Great Mutiny was of such character that national pride along with views of policy would fain shade it off into the historical background. Such events can not be ignored, but there is a considerate way of historically treating them. If a well-constituted individual refrains from blazoning aught amiss or calamitous in his family, a nation in the like circumstance may without reproach be equally discreet.

Though after parleyings between government and the ringleaders, and concessions by the former as to some glaring abuses, the first uprising—that at Spithead—with difficulty was put down, or matters for the time pacified; yet at the Nore the unforeseen renewal of insurrection on a yet larger scale, and emphasized in the conferences that ensued by demands deemed by the authorities not only inadmissible but aggressively insolent, indicated—if the Red Flag did not sufficiently do so—what was the spirit animating the men. Final suppression, however, there was; but only made possible perhaps by the unswerving loyalty of the marine corps and voluntary resumption of loyalty among influential sections of the crews.

To some extent the Nore Mutiny may be regarded as analogous to the distempering irruption of contagious fever in a frame constitutionally sound, and which anon throws it off.

At all events, of these thousands of mutineers were some of the tars who not so very long afterwards—whether wholly prompted thereto by patriotism, or pugnacious instinct, or by both—helped to win a coronet for Nelson at the Nile, and the naval crown of crowns for him at Trafalgar. To the mutineers those battles and especially Trafalgar were a plenary absolution and a grand one. For all that goes to make up scenic naval display and heroic magnificence in arms, those battles, especially Trafalgar, stand unmatched in human annals.

4

In this matter of writing, resolve as one may to keep to the main road, some bypaths have an enticement not readily to be withstood. I am going to err into such a bypath. If the reader will keep me company I shall be glad. At the least, we can promise ourselves that pleasure which is wickedly said to be in sinning, for a literary sin the divergence will be.

Very likely it is no new remark that the inventions of our time have at last brought about a change in sea warfare in degree corresponding to the revolution in all warfare effected by the original introduction from China into Europe of gunpowder. The first European firearm, a clumsy contrivance, was, as is well known, scouted by no few of the knights as a base implement, good enough peradventure for weavers too craven to stand up crossing steel with steel in frank fight. But as ashore knightly valor, though shorn of its blazonry, did not cease with the knights, neither on the seas—though nowadays in encounters there a certain kind of displayed gallantry be fallen out of date as hardly applicable under changed circumstances—did the nobler qualities of such naval magnates as Don John of Austria, Doria, Van Tromp, Jean Bart, the long line of British Admirals and the American Decaturs of 1812 become obsolete with their wooden walls.

Nevertheless, to anybody who can hold the Present at its worth without being inappreciative of the Past, it may be forgiven, if to such an one the solitary old hulk at Portsmouth, Nelson's *Victory*, seems to float there, not alone as the decaying monument of a fame incorruptible, but also as a poetic reproach, softened by its picturesqueness, to the *Monitors* and yet mightier hulls of the European ironclads. And this not altogether because such craft are unsightly, unavoidably lacking the symmetry and grand lines of the old battleships, but equally for other reasons.

There are some, perhaps, who while not altogether inaccessible to that poetic reproach just alluded to, may yet on behalf of the new order be disposed to parry it; and this to the extent of iconoclasm, if need be. For example, prompted by the sight of the star inserted in the *Victory*'s quarter-deck designating the spot where the Great Sailor fell, these martial utilitarians may suggest considerations implying that Nelson's ornate publication of his person in battle was not only unnecessary, but not military, nay, savored of foolhardiness and vanity. They may add, too, that at Trafalgar it was in effect nothing less than a challenge to death; and death came; and that but for his bravado the victorious admiral might possibly have survived the battle, and so, instead of having his sagacious dying injunctions overruled by his immediate successor in command, he himself when the contest was decided might have brought his shattered fleet to anchor, a proceeding which might have averted the deplorable loss of life by shipwreck in the elemental tempest that followed the martial one.

Well, should we set aside the more disputable point whether for various reasons it was possible to anchor the fleet, then plausibly enough the Benthamites of war may urge the above. But the *might-have-been* is but boggy ground to build on. And, certainly, in foresight as to the larger issue of an encounter, and anxious preparations for it—buoying the deadly way and mapping it out, as at Copenhagen—few commanders have been so painstakingly circumspect as this same reckless declarer of his person in fight.

Personal prudence, even when dictated by quite other than selfish considerations, surely is no special virtue in a military man; while an excessive love of glory, impassioning a less burning impulse, the honest sense of duty, is the first. If the name *Wellington* is not so much of a trumpet to the blood as the simpler name *Nelson*, the reason for this may perhaps be inferred from the above. Alfred in his funeral ode on the victor of Waterloo ventures not to call him the greatest soldier of all time, though in the same ode he invokes Nelson as "the greatest sailor since our world began."

At Trafalgar, Nelson on the brink of opening the fight sat down and wrote his last brief will and testament. If under the presentiment of the most magnificent of all victories to be crowned by his own glorious death, a sort of priestly motive led him to dress his person in the jewelled vouchers of his own shining deeds; if thus to have adorned himself for the altar and the sacrifice were indeed vainglory, then affectation and fustian is each more heroic line in the great epics and dramas, since in such lines the poet but embodies in verse those exaltations of sentiment that a nature like Nelson, the opportunity being given, vitalizes into acts.

5

Yes, the outbreak at the Nore was put down. But not every grievance was redressed. If the contractors, for example, were no longer permitted to ply some practices peculiar to their tribe everywhere, such as providing shoddy cloth, rations not sound, or false in the measure; not the less impressment, for one thing, went on. By custom sanctioned for centuries, and judicially maintained by a Lord Chancellor as late as Mansfield, that mode of manning the fleet, a mode now fallen into a sort of abeyance but never formally renounced, it was not practicable to give up in those years. Its abrogation would have crippled the indispensable fleet, one wholly under canvas, no steam power, its innumerable sails and thousands of cannon, everything in short, worked by muscle alone; a fleet the more insatiate in demand for men, because then multiplying its ships of all grades against contingencies present and to come of the convulsed Continent.

Discontent foreran the Two Mutinies, and more or less it lurkingly survived them. Hence it was not unreasonable to apprehend some return of trouble, sporadic or general. One instance of such apprehensions: In the same year with this story, Nelson, then Rear Admiral Sir Horatio, being with the fleet off the Spanish coast, was directed by the admiral in command to shift his pennant from the *Captain* to the *Theseus*; and for this reason: that the latter ship having newly arrived on the station from home, where it had taken part in the Great Mutiny, danger was apprehended from the temper of the men; and it was thought that an officer like Nelson was the one, not indeed to terrorize the crew into base subjection, but to win them, by force of his mere presence and heroic personality, back to an allegiance if not as enthusiastic as his own yet as true. So it was that for a time on more than one quarter-deck, anxiety did exist. At sea, precautionary vigilance was strained against relapse. At short notice an engagement might come on. When it did, the lieutenants assigned to batteries felt it incumbent on them, in some instances, to stand with drawn swords behind the men working the guns.

6

But on board the seventy-four in which Billy now swung his hammock, very little in the manner of the men and nothing obvious in the demeanor of the officers would have suggested to an ordinary observer that the Great Mutiny was a recent event. In their general bearing and conduct the commissioned officers of a warship naturally take their tone from the commander, that is if he have that ascendancy of character that ought to be his.

Captain the Honorable Edward Fairfax Vere, to give his full title, was a bachelor of forty or thereabouts, a sailor of distinction even in a time prolific of renowned seamen. Though allied to the higher nobility, his advancement had not been altogether owing to influences connected with that circumstance. He had seen much service, been in various engagements, always acquitting himself as an officer mindful of the welfare of his men, but never tolerating an infraction of discipline; thoroughly versed in the science of his profession, and intrepid to the verge of temerity, though never injudiciously so. For his gallantry in the West Indian waters as flag lieutenant under Rodney in that admiral's crowning victory over De Grasse, he was made a post captain.

Ashore, in the garb of a civilian, scarce anyone would have taken him for a sailor, more especially that he never garnished unprofessional talk with nautical terms, and grave in his bearing, evinced little appreciation of mere humor. It was not out of keeping with these traits that on a passage when nothing demanded his paramount action, he was the most undemonstrative of men. Any landsman observing this gentleman not conspicuous by his stature and wearing no pronounced insignia, emerging from his cabin to the open deck, and noting the silent deference of the officers retiring to leeward, might have taken him for the King's guest, a civilian aboard the King's ship, some highly honorable discreet envoy on his way to an important post. But in fact this unobtrusiveness of demeanor may have proceeded from a certain unaffected modesty of manhood sometimes accompanying a resolute nature, a modesty evinced at all times not calling for pronounced action, and which shown in any rank of life suggests a virtue aristocratic in kind. As with some others engaged in various departments of the world's more heroic activities, Captain Vere though practical enough upon occasion would at times betray a certain dreaminess of mood. Standing alone on the weather side of the quarter-deck, one hand holding by the rigging, he would absently gaze off at the blank sea. At the presentation to him then of some minor matter interrupting the current of his thoughts he would show more or less irascibility; but instantly he would control it.

In the navy he was popularly known by the appellation "Starry Vere." How such a designation happened to fall upon one who whatever his sterling qualities was without any brilliant ones, was in this wise: A favorite kinsman, Lord Denton, a freehearted fellow, had been the first to meet and congratulate him upon his return to England from his West Indian cruise; and but the day previous turning over a copy of Andrew Marvell's poems had lighted, not for the first time, however, upon the lines entitled "Appleton House," the name of one of the seats of their common ancestor, a hero in the German wars of the seventeenth century, in which poem occur the lines:

> This 'tis to have been from the first
> In a domestic heaven nursed,
> Under the discipline severe
> Of Fairfax and the starry Vere.

And so, upon embracing his cousin fresh from Rodney's great victory wherein he had played so gallant a part, brimming over with just family pride in the sailor of their house, he exuberantly exclaimed, "Give ye joy, Ed; give ye joy, my starry Vere!" This got currency, and the novel prefix serving in familiar parlance readily to distinguish the *Bellipotent*'s captain from another Vere his senior, a distant relative, an officer of like rank in the navy, it remained permanently attached to the surname.

7

In view of the part that the commander of the *Bellipotent* plays in scenes shortly to follow, it may be well to fill out that sketch of his outlined in the previous chapter.

Aside from his qualities as a sea-officer Captain Vere was an exceptional character. Unlike no few of England's renowned sailors, long and arduous service with signal devotion to it had not resulted in absorbing and *salting* the entire man. He had a marked leaning toward everything intellectual. He loved books, never going to sea without a newly replenished library, compact but of the best. The isolated leisure, in some cases so wearisome, falling at intervals to commanders even during a war cruise, never was tedious to Captain Vere. With nothing of that literary taste which less heeds the thing conveyed than the vehicle, his bias was toward those books to which every serious mind of superior order occupying any active post of authority in the world naturally inclines: books treating of actual men and events no matter of what era—history, biography and unconventional writers like Montaigne, who, free from cant and convention, honestly and in the spirit of common sense philosophize upon realities. In this line of reading he found confirmation of his own more reasoned thoughts—confirmation which he had vainly sought in social converse, so that as touching most fundamental topics, there had got to be established in him some positive convictions which he forefelt would abide in him essentially unmodified so long as his intelligent part remained unimpaired. In view of the troubled period in which his lot was cast, this was well for him. His settled convictions were as a dyke against those invading waters of novel opinion social, political and otherwise, which carried away as in a torrent no few minds in those days, minds by nature not inferior to his own. While other members of that aristocracy to which by birth he belonged were incensed at the innovators mainly because their theories were inimical to the privileged classes, not alone Captain Vere disinterestedly opposed them not alone because they seemed to him incapable of embodiment in lasting institutions, but at war with the peace of the world and the true welfare of mankind.

With minds less stored than his and less earnest, some officers of his rank, with whom at times he would necessarily consort, found him lacking in the companionable quality, a dry and bookish gentleman, as they deemed. Upon any chance withdrawal from their company one would be apt to say to another, something like this: "Vere is a noble fellow, Starry Vere. Spite the gazettes, Sir Horatio" (meaning him who became Lord Nelson) "is at bottom scarce a better seaman or fighter. But between you and me now, don't you think there is a queer streak of the pedantic running through him? Yes, like the King's yarn in a coil of navy rope?"

Some apparent ground there was for this sort of confidential criticism; since not only did the captain's discourse never fall into the jocosely familiar, but in illustrating of any point touching the stirring personages and events of the time he would be as apt to cite some historic character or incident of antiquity as that he would cite from the moderns. He seemed unmindful of the circumstance that to his bluff company such remote allusions, however pertinent they might really be, were altogether alien to men whose reading was mainly confined to the journals. But considerateness in such matters is not easy to natures constituted like Captain Vere's. Their honesty prescribes to them directness, sometimes far-reaching like that of a migratory fowl that in its flight never heeds when it crosses a frontier.

8

The lieutenants and other commissioned gentlemen forming Captain Vere's staff it is not necessary here to particularize, nor needs it to make any mention of any of the warrant officers. But among the petty officers was one who having much to do with the story, may as well be forthwith introduced. His portrait I essay, but shall never hit it. This was John Claggart, the master-at-arms. But that sea title may to landsmen seem somewhat equivocal. Originally, doubtless, that petty officer's function was the instruction of the men in the use of arms, sword or cutlas. But very long ago, owing to the advance in gunnery making hand-to-hand encounters less frequent and giving to nitre and sulphur the pre-eminence over steel, that function ceased; the master-at-arms of a great war-ship becoming a sort of chief of police, charged among other matters with the duty of preserving order on the populous lower gun decks.

Claggart was a man about five-and-thirty, somewhat spare and tall, yet of no ill figure upon the whole. His hand was too small and shapely to have been accustomed to hard toil. The face was a notable one, the features all except the chin cleanly cut as those on a Greek medallion; yet the chin, beardless as Tecumseh's, had something of strange protuberant broadness in its make that recalled the prints of the Reverend Dr. Titus Oates, the historic deponent with the clerical drawl in the time of Charles II and the fraud of the alleged Popish Plot. It served Claggart in his office that his eye could cast a tutoring glance. His brow was of the sort phrenologically associated with more than average intellect; silken jet curls partly clustering over it, making a foil to the pallor below, a pallor tinged with a faint shade of amber akin to the hue of time-tinted marbles of old. This complexion, singularly contrasting with the red or deeply bronzed visages of the sailors, and in part the result of his official seclusion from the sunlight, though it was not exactly displeasing, nevertheless seemed to hint of something defective or abnormal in the constitution and blood. But his general aspect and manner were so suggestive of an education and career incongruous with his naval function that when not actively engaged in it he looked a man of high quality, social and moral, who for reasons of his own was keeping incog. Nothing was known of his former life. It might be that he was an Englishman; and yet there lurked a bit of accent in his speech suggesting that possibly he was not such by birth, but through naturalization in early childhood. Among certain grizzled sea gossips of the gun decks and forecastle went a rumor perdue that the master-at-arms was a *chevalier* who had volunteered into the King's navy by way of compounding for some mysterious swindle whereof he had been arraigned at the King's Bench. The fact that nobody could substantiate this report was, of course, nothing against its secret currency. Such a rumor once started on the gun decks in reference to almost anyone below the rank of a commissioned officer would, during the period assigned to this narrative, have seemed not altogether wanting in credibility to the tarry old wiseacres of a man-of-war crew. And indeed a man of Claggart's accomplishments, without prior nautical experience, entering the navy at mature life, as he did, and necessarily allotted at the start to the lowest grade in it; a man too who never made allusion to his previous life ashore; these were circumstances which in the dearth of exact knowledge as to his true antecedents opened to the invidious a vague field for unfavorable surmise.

But the sailors' dog watch gossip concerning him derived a vague plausibility from the fact that now for some period the British navy could so little afford to be squeamish in the matter of keeping up the muster-rolls, that not only were press gangs notoriously abroad both afloat and ashore, but there was little or no secret about another matter, namely, that the London police were at liberty to capture any able-bodied suspect, any questionable fellow at large, and summarily ship him to dockyard or fleet. Furthermore, even among voluntary enlistments there were instances where the motive thereto partook neither of patriotic impulse nor yet of a random desire to experience a bit of sea life and martial adventure. Insolvent debtors of minor grade, together with the promiscuous lame ducks of morality, found in the navy a convenient and secure refuge, secure because once enlisted aboard a King's ship, they were as much in sanctuary as the transgressor of the Middle Ages harboring himself under the shadow of the altar. Such sanctioned irregularities, which for obvious reasons the government would hardly think to parade at the time and which consequently, and as affecting the least influential class of mankind, have all but dropped into oblivion, lend color to something for the truth whereof I do not vouch, and hence have some scruple in stating; something I remember having seen in print though the book I can not recall; but the same thing was personally communicated to me now more than forty years ago by an old pensioner in a cocked hat with whom I had a most interesting talk on the terrace at Greenwich, a Baltimore Negro, a Trafalgar man. It was to this effect: In the case of a war-ship short of hands whose speedy sailing was imperative, the deficient quota, in lack of any other way of making it good, would be eked out by draughts culled direct from the jails. For reasons previously suggested it would not perhaps be easy at the present day directly to prove or disprove the allegation. But allowed as a verity, how significant would it be of England's straits at the time confronted by those wars which like a flight of harpies rose shrieking from the din and dust of the fallen Bastille. That era appears measurably clear to us who look back at it, and but read of it. But to the grandfathers of us graybeards, the more thoughtful of them, the genius of it presented an aspect like that of Camoëns' Spirit of the Cape, an eclipsing menace mysterious and prodigious. Not America was exempt from apprehension. At the height of Napoleon's unexampled conquests, there were Americans who had fought at Bunker Hill who looked forward to the possibility that the Atlantic might prove no barrier against the ultimate schemes of this French portentous upstart from the revolutionary chaos who seemed in act of fulfilling judgement prefigured in the Apocalypse.

But the less credence was to be given to the gun-deck talk touching Claggart, seeing that no man holding his office in a man-of-war can ever hope to be popular with the crew. Besides, in derogatory comments upon anyone against whom they have a grudge, or for any reason or no reason mislike, sailors are much like landsmen: they are apt to exaggerate or romance it.

About as much was really known to the *Bellipotent*'s tars of the master-at-arms' career before entering the service as an astronomer knows about a comet's travels prior to its first observable appearance in the sky. The verdict of the sea quidnuncs has been cited only by way of showing what sort of moral impression the man made upon rude uncultivated natures whose conceptions of human wickedness were necessarily of the narrowest, limited to ideas of vulgar rascality—a thief among the swinging hammocks during a night watch, or the man brokers and land-sharks of the seaports.

It was no gossip, however, but fact that though, as before hinted, Claggart upon his entrance into the navy was, as a novice, assigned to the least honorable section of a man-of-war's crew, embracing the drudgery, he did not long remain there. The superior capacity he immediately evinced, his constitutional sobriety, an ingratiating deference to superiors, together with a peculiar ferreting genius manifested on a singular occasion; all this, capped by a certain austere patriotism, abruptly advanced him to the position of master-at-arms.

Of this maritime chief of police the ship's corporals, so called, were the immediate subordinates, and compliant ones; and this, as is to be noted in some business departments ashore, almost to a degree inconsistent with entire moral volition. His place put various converging wires of underground influence under the chief's control, capable when astutely worked through his understrappers of operating to the mysterious discomfort, if nothing worse, of any of the sea commonalty.

9

Life in the foretop well agreed with Billy Budd. There, when not actually engaged on the yards yet higher aloft, the topmen, who as such had been picked out for youth and activity, constituted an aerial club lounging at ease against the smaller stun'sails rolled up into cushions, spinning yarns like the lazy gods, and frequently amused with what was going on in the busy world of the decks below. No wonder then that a young fellow of Billy's disposition was well content in such society. Giving no cause of offence to anybody, he was always alert at a call. So in the merchant service it had been with him. But now such a punctiliousness in duty was shown that his topmates would sometimes good-naturedly laugh at him for it. This heightened alacrity had its cause, namely, the impression made upon him by the first formal gangway-punishment he had ever witnessed, which befell the day following his impressment. It had been incurred by a little fellow, young, a novice, an after-guardsman absent from his assigned post when the ship was being put about; a dereliction resulting in a rather serious hitch to that maneuvre, one demanding instantaneous promptitude in letting go and making fast. When Billy saw the culprit's naked back under the scourge, gridironed with red welts, and worse, when he marked the dire expression on the liberated man's face as with his woolen shirt flung over him by the executioner he rushed forward from the spot to bury himself in the crowd, Billy was horrified. He resolved that never through remissness would he make himself liable to such a visitation or do or omit aught that might merit even verbal reproof. What then was his surprise and concern when ultimately he found himself getting into petty trouble occasionally about such matters as the stowage of his bag or something amiss in his hammock, matters under the police oversight of the ship's corporals of the lower decks, and which brought down on him a vague threat from one of them.

So heedful in all things as he was, how could this be? He could not understand it, and it more than vexed him. When he spoke to his young topmates about it they were either lightly incredulous or found something comical in his unconcealed anxiety. "Is it your bag, Billy?" said one. "Well, sew yourself up in it, bully boy, and then you'll be sure to know if anybody meddles with it."

Now there was a veteran aboard who because his years began to disqualify him for more active work had been recently assigned duty as mainmastman in his watch, looking to the gear belayed at the rail roundabout that great spar near the deck. At off-times the Foretopman had picked up some acquaintance with him, and now in his trouble it occurred to him that he might be the sort of person to go to for wise counsel. He was an old Dansker long anglicized in the service, of few words, many wrinkles and some honorable scars. His wizened face, time-tinted and weather-stained to the complexion of an antique parchment, was here and there peppered blue by the chance explosion of a gun cartridge in action. He was an *Agamemnon* man; some two years prior to the time of this story having served under Nelson when but still captain in that ship immortal in naval memory, which dismantled and in part broken up to her bare ribs is seen a grand skeleton in Haden's etching. As one of a boarding party from the *Agamemnon* he had received a cut slantwise along one temple and cheek leaving a long scar like a streak of dawn's light falling athwart the dark visage. It was on account of that scar and the affair in which it was known that he had received it, as well as from his blue-peppered complexion, that the Dansker went among the *Bellipotent*'s crew by the name of "Board-Her-in-the-Smoke."

Now the first time that his small weasel eyes happened to light on Billy Budd, a certain grim internal merriment set all his ancient wrinkles into antic play. Was it that his eccentric unsentimental old sapience, primitive in its kind, saw or thought it saw something which in contrast with the war-ship's environment looked oddly incongruous in the Handsome Sailor? But after slyly studying him at intervals, the old Merlin's equivocal merriment was modified; for now when the twain would meet, it would start in his face a quizzing sort of look, but it would be but momentary and sometimes replaced by an expression of speculative query as to what might eventually befall a nature like that, dropped into a world not without some man-traps and against whose subtleties simple courage lacking experience and address, and without any touch of defensive ugliness, is of little avail; and where such innocence as man is capable of does yet in a moral emergency not always sharpen the faculties or enlighten the will.

However it was, the Dansker in his ascetic way rather took to Billy. Nor was this only because of a certain philosophic interest in such a character. There was another cause. While the old man's eccentricities, sometimes bordering on the ursine, repelled the juniors, Billy, undeterred thereby, revering him as a salt hero, would make advances, never passing the old *Agamemnon* man without a salutation marked by that respect which is seldom lost on the aged, however crabbed at times or whatever their station in life.

There was a vein of dry humor, or what not, in the mastman; and, whether in freak of patriarchal irony touching Billy's youth and athletic frame, or for some other and more recondite reason, from the first in addressing him he always substituted *Baby* for Billy. The Dansker in fact being the originator of the name by which the foretopman eventually became known aboard ship.

Well then, in his mysterious little difficulty going in quest of the wrinkled one, Billy found him off duty in a dogwatch ruminating by himself, seated on a shot box of the upper gun deck, now and then surveying with a somewhat cynical regard certain of the more swaggering promenaders there. Billy recounted his trouble, again wondering how it all happened. The salt seer attentively listened, accompanying the foretopman's recital with queer twitchings of his wrinkles and problematical little sparkles of his small ferret eyes. Making an end of his story, the foretopman asked, "And now, Dansker, do tell me what you think of it."

The old man, shoving up the front of his tarpaulin and deliberately rubbing the long slant scar at the point where it entered the thin hair, laconically said, "Baby Budd, *Jemmy Legs*" (meaning the master-at-arms) "is down on you."

"*Jemmy Legs!*" ejaculated Billy, his welkin eyes expanding. "What for? Why he calls me 'the sweet and pleasant fellow,' they tell me."

"Does he so?" grinned the grizzled one; then said, "Ay, Baby lad, a sweet voice has Jemmy Legs."

"No, not always. But to me he has. I seldom pass him but there comes a pleasant word."

"And that's because he's down upon you, Baby Budd."

Such reiteration, along with the manner of it, incomprehensible to a novice, disturbed Billy almost as much as the mystery for which he had sought explanation. Something less unpleasingly oracular he tried to extract; but the old sea Chiron, thinking perhaps that for the nonce he had sufficiently instructed his young Achilles, pursed his lips, gathered all his wrinkles together, and would commit himself to nothing further.

Years, and those experiences which befall certain shrewder men subordinated lifelong to the will of superiors, all this had developed in the Dansker the pithy guarded cynicism that was his leading characteristic.

10

The next day an incident served to confirm Billy Budd in his incredulity as to the Dansker's strange summing up of the case submitted. The ship at noon, going large before the wind, was rolling on her course, and he, below at dinner and engaged in some sportful talk with the members of his mess, chanced in a sudden lurch to spill the entire contents of his soup pan upon the new scrubbed deck. Claggart, the master-at-arms, official rattan in hand, happened to be passing along the battery in a bay of which the mess was lodged, and the greasy liquid streamed just across his path. Stepping over it, he was proceeding on his way without comment, since the matter was nothing to take notice of under the circumstances, when he happened to observe who it was that had done the spilling. His countenance changed. Pausing, he was about to ejaculate something hasty at the sailor, but checked himself, and pointing down to the streaming soup, playfully tapped him from behind with his rattan, saying in a low musical voice peculiar to him at times, "Handsomely done, my lad! And handsome is as handsome did it too!" And with that passed on. Not noted by Billy, as not coming within his view, was the involuntary smile, or rather grimace, that accompanied Claggart's equivocal words. Aridly it drew down the thin corners of his shapely mouth. But everybody taking his remark as meant for humourous, and at which therefore as coming from a superior they were bound to laugh "with counterfeited glee," acted accordingly; and Billy tickled, it may be, by the allusion to his being the handsome sailor, merrily joined in; then addressing his messmates exclaimed, "There now, who says that Jemmy Legs is down on me!" "And who said he was, Beauty?" demanded one Donald with some surprise. Whereat the foretopman looked a little foolish, recalling that it was only one person, *Board-Her-in-the-Smoke*, who had suggested what to him was the smoky idea that this master-at-arms was in any peculiar way hostile to him. Meantime that functionary, resuming his path, must have momentarily worn some expression less guarded than that of the bitter smile, and usurping the face from the heart, some distorting expression perhaps; for a drummerboy heedlessly frolicking along from the opposite direction and chancing to come into light collision with his person was strangely disconcerted by his aspect. Nor was the impression lessened when the official, impulsively giving him a sharp cut with the rattan, vehemently exclaimed, "Look where you go!"

11

What was the matter with the master-at-arms? And, be the matter what it might, how could it have direct relation to Billy Budd with whom, prior to the affair of the spilled soup, he had never come into any special contact, official or otherwise? What indeed could the trouble have to do with one so little inclined to give offence as the merchant ship's "peacemaker," even him who in Claggart's own phrase was "the sweet and pleasant young fellow"? Yes, why should Jemmy Legs, to borrow the Dansker's expression, be "down" on the Handsome Sailor? But, at heart and not for nothing, as the late chance encounter may indicate to the discerning, down on him, secretly down on him, he assuredly was.

Now to invent something touching the more private career of Claggart, something involving Billy Budd, of which something the latter should be wholly ignorant, some romantic incident implying that Claggart's knowledge of the young bluejacket began at some period anterior to catching sight of him on board the seventy-four—all this, not so difficult to do, might avail in a way more or less interesting to account for whatever of enigma may appear to lurk in the case. But in fact there was nothing of the sort. And yet the cause necessarily to be assumed as the sole one assignable is in its very realism as much charged with that prime element of Radcliffian romance, the mysterious, as any that the ingenuity of the author of the *Mysteries of Udolpho* could devise. For what can more partake of the mysterious than an antipathy spontaneous and profound such as is evoked in certain exceptional mortals by the mere aspect of some other mortal, however harmless he may be, if not called forth by this very harmlessness itself?

Now there can exist no irritating juxtaposition of dissimilar personalities comparable to that which is possible aboard a great war-ship fully manned and at sea. There, every day among all ranks, almost every man comes into more or less of contact with almost every other man. Wholly there to avoid even the sight of an aggravating object one must needs give it Jonah's toss or jump overboard himself. Imagine how all this might eventually operate on some peculiar human creature the direct reverse of a saint!

But for the adequate comprehending of Claggart by a normal nature these hints are insufficient. To pass from a normal nature to him one must cross "the deadly space between." And this is best done by indirection.

Long ago an honest scholar my senior, said to me in reference to one who like himself is now no more, a man so unimpeachably respectable that against him nothing was ever openly said though among the few something was whispered, "Yes, X— is a nut not to be cracked by the tap of a lady's fan. You are aware that I am the adherent of no organized religion, much less of any philosophy built into a system. Well, for all that, I think that to try and get into X—, enter his labyrinth and get out again, without a clue derived from some source other than what is known as 'knowledge of the world'—that were hardly possible, at least for me."

"Why," said I, "X—, however singular a study to some, is yet human, and knowledge of the world assuredly implies the knowledge of human nature, and in most of its varieties."

"Yes, but a superficial knowledge of it, serving ordinary purposes. But for anything deeper, I am not certain whether to know the world and to know human nature be not two distinct branches of knowledge, which while they may coexist in the same heart, yet either may exist with little or nothing of the other. Nay, in an average man of the world, his constant rubbing with it blunts that fine spiritual insight indispensable to the understanding of the essential in certain exceptional characters, whether evil ones or good. In a matter of some importance I have seen a girl wind an old lawyer about her little finger. Nor was it the dotage of senile love. Nothing of the sort. But he knew law better than he knew the girl's heart. Coke and Blackstone hardly shed so much light into obscure spiritual places as the Hebrew prophets. And who were they? Mostly recluses."

At the time, my inexperience was such that I did not quite see the drift of all this. It may be that I see it now. And, indeed, if that lexicon which is based on Holy Writ were any longer popular, one might with less difficulty define and denominate certain phenomenal men. As it is, one must turn to some authority not liable to the charge of being tinctured with the biblical element.

In a list of definitions included in the authentic translation of Plato, a list attributed to him, occurs this: "Natural Depravity: a depravity according to nature," a definition which though savoring of Calvinism, by no means involves Calvin's dogma as to total mankind. Evidently its intent makes it applicable but to individuals. Not many are the examples of this depravity which the gallows and jail supply. At any rate for notable instances, since these have no vulgar alloy of the brute in them, but invariably are dominated by intellectuality, one must go elsewhere. Civilization, especially if of the austerer sort, is auspicious to it. It folds itself in the mantle of respectability. It has its certain negative virtues serving as silent auxiliaries. It never allows wine to get within its guard. It is not going too far to say that it is without vices or small sins. There is a phenomenal pride in it that excludes them. It is never mercenary or avaricious. In short the depravity here meant partakes nothing of the sordid or sensual. It is serious, but free from acerbity. Though no flatterer of mankind it never speaks ill of it.

But the thing which in eminent instances signalizes so exceptional a nature is this: Though the man's even temper and discreet bearing would seem to intimate a mind peculiarly subject to the law of reason, not the less in his heart he would seem to riot in complete exemption from that law, having apparently little to do with reason further than to employ it as an ambidexter implement for effecting the irrational. That is to say: Toward the accomplishment of an aim which in wantonness of malignity would seem to partake of the insane, he will direct a cool judgement sagacious and sound. These men are madmen, and of the most dangerous sort, for their lunacy is not continuous, but occasional, evoked by some special object; it is probably secretive, which is as much to say it is self-contained, so that when, moreover, most active it is to the average mind not distinguishable from sanity, and for the reason above suggested: that whatever its aims may be—and the aim is never declared—the method and the outward proceeding are always perfectly rational.

Now something such an one was Claggart, in whom was the mania of an evil nature, not engendered by vicious training or corrupting books or licentious living, but born with him and innate, in short "a depravity according to nature."

Dark sayings are these, some will say. But why? Is it because they somewhat savor of Holy Writ in its phrase "mysteries of iniquity"? If they do, such savor was far from being intended, for little will it commend these pages to many a reader of to-day.

The point of the present story turning on the hidden nature of the master-at-arms has necessitated this chapter. With an added hint or two in connection with the incident at the mess, the resumed narrative must be left to vindicate, as it may, its own credibility.

12

That Claggart's figure was not amiss, and his face, save the chin, well moulded, has already been said. Of these favorable points he seemed not insensible, for he was not only neat but careful in his dress. But the form of Billy Budd was heroic; and if his face was without the intellectual look of the pallid Claggart's, not the less was it lit, like his, from within, though from a different source. The bonfire in his heart made luminous the rose-tan in his cheek.

In view of the marked contrast between the persons of the twain, it is more than probable that when the master-at-arms in the scene last given applied to the sailor the proverb "Handsome is as handsome does," he there let escape an ironic inkling, not caught by the young sailors who heard it, as to what it was that had first moved him against Billy, namely, his significant personal beauty.

Now envy and antipathy, passions irreconcilable in reason, nevertheless in fact may spring conjoined like Chang and Eng in one birth. Is Envy then such a monster? Well, though many an arraigned mortal has in hopes of mitigated penalty pleaded guilty to horrible actions, did ever anybody seriously confess to envy? Something there is in it universally felt to be more shameful than even felonious crime. And not only does everybody disown it, but the better sort are inclined to incredulity when it is in earnest imputed to an intelligent man. But since its lodgement is in the heart not the brain, no degree of intellect supplies a guarantee against it. But Claggart's was no vulgar form of the passion. Nor, as directed toward Billy Budd, did it partake of that streak of apprehensive jealousy that marred Saul's visage perturbedly brooding on the comely young David. Claggart's envy struck deeper. If askance he eyed the good looks, cheery health, and frank enjoyment of young life in Billy Budd, it was because these went along with a nature that, as Claggart magnetically felt, had in its simplicity never willed malice or experienced the reactionary bite of that serpent. To him, the spirit lodged within Billy, and looking out from his welkin eyes as from windows, that ineffability it was which made the dimple in his dyed cheek, suppled his joints, and dancing in his yellow curls made him pre-eminently the Handsome Sailor. One person excepted, the master-at-arms was perhaps the only man in the ship intellectually capable of adequately appreciating the moral phenomenon presented in Billy Budd. And the insight but intensified his passion, which assuming various secret forms within him, at times assumed that of cynic disdain—disdain of innocence—to be nothing more than innocent! Yet in an aesthetic way he saw the charm of it, the courageous free-and-easy temper of it, and fain would have shared it, but he despaired of it.

With no power to annul the elemental evil in him, though readily enough he could hide it; apprehending the good, but powerless to be it; a nature like Claggart's, surcharged with energy as such natures almost invariably are, what recourse is left to it but to recoil upon itself and like the scorpion for which the Creator alone is responsible, act out to the end the part allotted it.

13

Passion, and passion in its profoundest, is not a thing demanding a palatial stage whereon to play its part. Down among the groundlings, among the beggars and rakers of the garbage, profound passion is enacted. And the circumstances that provoke it, however trivial or mean, are no measure of its power. In the present instance the stage is a scrubbed gun deck, and one of the external provocations a man-of-war's man's spilled soup.

Now when the master-at-arms noticed whence came that greasy fluid streaming before his feet, he must have taken it—to some extent wilfully, perhaps—not for the mere accident it assuredly was, but for the sly escape of a spontaneous feeling on Billy's part more or less answering to the antipathy on his own. In effect a foolish demonstration, he must have thought, and very harmless, like the futile kick of a heifer, which yet were the heifer a shod stallion would not be so harmless. Even so was it that into the gall of Claggart's envy he infused the vitriol of his contempt. But the incident confirmed to him certain telltale reports purveyed to his ear by "Squeak," one of his more cunning corporals, a grizzled little man, so nicknamed by the sailors on account of his squeaky voice and sharp visage ferreting about the dark corners of the lower decks after interlopers, satirically suggesting to them the idea of a rat in a cellar.

From his chief's employing him as an implicit tool in laying little traps for the worriment of the foretopman—for it was from the master-at-arms that the petty persecutions heretofore adverted to had proceeded—the corporal having naturally enough concluded that his master could have no love for the sailor, made it his business, faithful understrapper that he was, to foment the ill blood by perverting to his chief certain innocent frolics of the goodnatured foretopman, besides inventing for his mouth sundry contumelious epithets he claimed to have overheard him let fall. The master-at-arms never suspected the veracity of these reports, more especially as to the epithets, for he well knew how secretly unpopular may become a master-at-arms, at least a master-at-arms of those days, zealous in his function, and how the bluejackets shoot at him in private their raillery and wit; the nickname by which he goes among them (Jemmy Legs) implying under the form of merriment their cherished disrespect and dislike. But in view of the greediness of hate for pabulum, it hardly needed a purveyor to feed Claggart's passion.

An uncommon prudence is habitual with the subtler depravity, for it has everything to hide. And in case of an injury but suspected, its secretiveness voluntarily cuts it off from enlightenment or disillusion; and, not unreluctantly, action is taken upon surmise as upon certainty. And the retaliation is apt to be in monstrous disproportion to the supposed offence; for when in anybody was revenge in its exactions aught else but an inordinate usurer? But how with Claggart's conscience? For though consciences are unlike as foreheads, every intelligence, not excluding the Scriptural devils who *"believe and tremble,"* has one. But Claggart's conscience being but the lawyer to his will, made ogres of trifles, probably arguing that the motive imputed to Billy in spilling the soup just when he did, together with the epithets alleged, these, if nothing more, made a strong case against him; nay, justified animosity into a sort of retributive righteousness. The Pharisee is the Guy Fawkes prowling in the hid chambers underlying the Claggarts. And they can really form no conception of an unreciprocated malice. Probably, the master-at-arms' clandestine persecution of Billy was started to try the temper of the man; but it had not developed any quality in him that enmity could make official use of or even pervert into plausible self-justification; so that the occurrence at the mess, petty if it were, was a welcome one to that peculiar conscience assigned to be the private mentor of Claggart; and, for the rest, not improbably it put him upon new experiments.

14

Not many days after the last incident narrated, something befell Billy Budd that more gravelled him than aught that had previously occurred.

It was a warm night for the latitude; and the foretopman, whose watch at the time was properly below, was dozing on the uppermost deck whither he had ascended from his hot hammock, one of hundreds suspended so closely wedged together over a lower gun deck that there was little or no swing to them. He lay as in the shadow of a hillside, stretched under the lee of the booms, a piled ridge of spare spars amidships between foremast and mainmast and among which the ship's largest boat, the launch, was stowed. Alongside of three other slumberers from below, he lay near that end of the booms which approaches the foremast; his station aloft on duty as a foretopman being just over the deck-station of the forecastlemen, entitling him according to usage to make himself more or less at home in that neighborhood.

Presently he was stirred into semiconsciousness by somebody, who must have previously sounded the sleep of the others, touching his shoulder, and then, as the foretopman raised his head, breathing into his ear in a quick whisper, "Slip into the lee forechains, Billy; there is something in the wind. Don't speak. Quick, I will meet you there," and disappearing.

Now Billy, like sundry other essentially good-natured ones, had some of the weaknesses inseparable from essential good nature; and among these was a reluctance, almost an incapacity of plumply saying *no* to an abrupt proposition not obviously absurd on the face of it, nor obviously unfriendly, nor iniquitous. And being of warm blood, he had not the phlegm tacitly to negative any proposition by unresponsive inaction. Like his sense of fear, his apprehension as to aught outside of the honest and natural was seldom very quick. Besides, upon the present occasion, the drowse from his sleep still hung upon him.

However it was, he mechanically rose, and sleepily wondering what could be in the wind, betook himself to the designated place, a narrow platform, one of six, outside of the high bulwarks and screened by the great deadeyes and multiple columned lanyards of the shrouds and back-stays; and, in a great warship of that time, of dimensions commensurate with the hull's magnitude; a tarry balcony in short, overhanging the sea, and so secluded that one mariner of the *Bellipotent*, a nonconformist old tar of a serious turn, made it even in daytime his private oratory.

In this retired nook the stranger soon joined Billy Budd. There was no moon as yet; a haze obscured the starlight. He could not distinctly see the stranger's face. Yet from something in the outline and carriage, Billy took him, and correctly, for one of the afterguard.

"Hist! Billy," said the man, in the same quick cautionary whisper as before. "You were impressed, weren't you? Well, so was I"; and he paused, as to mark the effect. But Billy, not knowing exactly what to make of this, said nothing. Then the other: "We are not the only impressed ones, Billy. There's a gang of us.—Couldn't you—help—at a pinch?"

"What do you mean?" demanded Billy, here thoroughly shaking off his drowse.

"Hist, hist!" the hurried whisper now growing husky. "See here," and the man held up two small objects faintly twinkling in the nightlight; "see, they are yours, Billy, if you'll only——"

But Billy broke in, and in his resentful eagerness to deliver himself his vocal infirmity somewhat intruded. "D–d–damme, I don't know what you are d–d–driving at, or what you mean, but you had better g–g–go where you belong!" For the moment the fellow, as confounded, did not stir; and Billy, springing to his feet, said, "If you d–don't start I'll t–t–toss you back over the r–rail!" There was no mistaking this and the mysterious emissary decamped, disappearing in the direction of the mainmast in the shadow of the booms.

"Hallo, what's the matter?" here came growling from a forecastleman awakened from his deck-doze by Billy's raised voice. And as the foretopman reappeared and was recognized by him: "Ah, Beauty, is it you? Well, some-thing must have been the matter for you st–st–stuttered."

"Oh," rejoined Billy, now mastering the impediment, "I found an afterguardsman in our part of the ship here, and I bid him be off where he belongs."

"And is that all you did about it, Foretopman?" gruffly demanded another, an irascible old fellow of brick-colored visage and hair who was known to his associate forecastlemen as "Red Pepper." "Such sneaks I should like to marry to the gunner's daughter!"—by that expression meaning that he would like to subject them to disciplinary castigation over a gun.

However, Billy's rendering of the matter satisfactorily accounted to these inquirers for the brief commotion, since of all the sections of a ship's company the forecastlemen, veterans for the most part and bigoted in their sea prejudices, are the most jealous in resenting territorial encroachments, especially on the part of any of the afterguard, of whom they have but a sorry opinion—chiefly landsmen, never going aloft except to reef or furl the mainsail, and in no wise competent to handle a marlinspike or turn in a deadeye, say.

15

This incident sorely puzzled Billy Budd. It was an entirely new experience, the first time in his life that he had ever been personally approached in underhand intriguing fashion. Prior to this encounter he had known nothing of the afterguardsman, the two men being stationed wide apart, one forward and aloft during his watch the other on deck and aft.

What could it mean? And could they really be guineas, those two glittering objects the interloper had held up to his eyes? Where could the fellow get guineas? Why, even spare buttons are not so plentiful at sea. The more he turned the matter over, the more he was nonplussed, and made uneasy and discomforted. In his disgustful recoil from an overture which, though he but ill comprehended he instinctively knew must involve evil of some sort, Billy Budd was like a young horse fresh from the pasture suddenly inhaling a vile whiff from some chemical factory, and by repeated snortings tries to get it out of his nostrils and lungs. This frame of mind barred all desire of holding further parley with the fellow, even were it but for the purpose of gaining some enlightenment as to his design in approaching him. And yet he was not without natural curiosity to see how such a visitor in the dark would look in broad day.

He espied him the following afternoon in his first dogwatch below, one of the smokers on that forward part of the upper gun deck allotted to the pipe. He recognized him by his general cut and build more than by his round freckled face and glassy eyes of pale blue, veiled with lashes all but white. And yet Billy was a bit uncertain whether indeed it were he—yonder chap about his own age chatting and laughing in freehearted way, leaning against a gun; a genial young fellow enough to look at, and something of a rattlebrain, to all appearance. Rather chubby too for a sailor, even an afterguardsman. In short the last man in the world, one would think, to be overburthened with thoughts, especially those perilous thoughts that must needs belong to a conspirator in any serious project, or even to the underling of such a conspirator.

Although Billy was not aware of it, the fellow, with a side-long watchful glance, had perceived Billy first, and then noting that Billy was looking at him, thereupon nodded a familiar sort of friendly recognition as to an old acquaintance, without interrupting the talk he was engaged in with the group of smokers. A day or two afterwards, chancing in the evening promenade on a gun deck to pass Billy, he offered a flying word of good-fellowship, as it were, which by its unexpectedness, and equivocalness under the circumstances, so embarrassed Billy that he knew not how to respond to it, and let it go unnoticed.

Billy was now left more at a loss than before. The ineffectual speculation into which he was led was so disturbingly alien to him that he did his best to smother it. It never entered his mind that here was a matter which from its extreme questionableness, it was his duty as a loyal bluejacket to report in the proper quarter. And, probably, had such a step been suggested to him, he would have been deterred from taking it by the thought, one of novice magnanimity, that it would savor overmuch of the dirty work of a telltale. He kept the thing to himself. Yet upon one occasion he could not forbear a little disburthening himself to the old Dansker, tempted thereto perhaps by the influence of a balmy night when the ship lay becalmed; the twain, silent for the most part, sitting together on deck, their heads propped against the bulwarks. But it was only a partial and anonymous account that Billy gave, the unfounded scruples above referred to preventing full disclosure to anybody. Upon hearing Billy's version, the sage Dansker seemed to divine more than he was told; and after a little meditation, during which his wrinkles were pursed as into a point, quite effacing for the time that quizzing expression his face sometimes wore: "Didn't I say so, Baby Budd?"

"Say what?" demanded Billy.

"Why, *Jemmy Legs* is down on you."

"And what," rejoined Billy in amazement, "has *Jemmy Legs* to do with that cracked afterguardsman?"

"Ho, it was an afterguardsman, then. A cat's-paw, a cat's-paw!" And with that exclamation, whether it had reference to a light puff of air just then coming over the calm sea, or subtler relation to the afterguardsman, there is no telling, the old Merlin gave a twisting wrench with his black teeth at his plug of tobacco, vouchsafing no reply to Billy's impetuous question, though now repeated, for it was his wont to relapse into grim silence when interrogated in skeptical sort as to any of his sententious oracles, not always very clear ones, rather partaking of that obscurity which invests most Delphic deliverances from any quarter.

Long experience had very likely brought this old man to that bitter prudence which never interferes in aught and never gives advice.

16

Yes, despite the Dansker's pithy insistence as to the master-at-arms being at the bottom of these strange experiences of Billy on board the *Bellipotent*, the young sailor was ready to ascribe them to almost anybody but the man who, to use Billy's own expression, "always had a pleasant word for him." This is to be wondered at. Yet not so much to be wondered at. In certain matters, some sailors even in mature life remain unsophisticated enough. But a young seafarer of the disposition of our athletic foretopman is much of a child-man. And yet a child's utter innocence is but its blank ignorance, and the innocence more or less wanes as intelligence waxes. But in Billy Budd intelligence, such as it was, had advanced while yet his simple-mindedness remained for the most part unaffected. Experience is a teacher indeed; yet did Billy's years make his experience small. Besides, he had none of that intuitive knowledge of the bad which in natures not good or incompletely so foreruns experience, and therefore may pertain, as in some instances it too clearly does pertain, even to youth.

And what could Billy know of man except of man as a mere sailor? And the old-fashioned sailor, the veritable man before the mast, the sailor from boyhood up, he, though indeed of the same species as a landsman, is in some respects singularly distinct from him. The sailor is frankness, the landsman is finesse. Life is not a game with the sailor, demanding the long head—no intricate game of chess where few moves are made in straightforwardness and ends are attained by indirection, an oblique, tedious, barren game hardly worth that poor candle burnt out in playing it.

Yes, as a class, sailors are in character a juvenile race. Even their deviations are marked by juvenility, this more especially holding true with the sailors of Billy's time. Then too, certain things which apply to all sailors do more pointedly operate here and there upon the junior one. Every sailor, too, is accustomed to obey orders without debating them; his life afloat is externally ruled for him; he is not brought into that promiscuous commerce with mankind where unobstructed free agency on equal terms—equal superficially, at least—soon teaches one that unless upon occasion he exercise a distrust keen in proportion to the fairness of the appearance, some foul turn may be served him. A ruled undemonstrative distrustfulness is so habitual, not with businessmen so much as with men who know their kind in less shallow relations than business, namely, certain men of the world, that they come at last to employ it all but unconsciously; and some of them would very likely feel real surprise at being charged with it as one of their general characteristics.

17

But after the little matter at the mess Billy Budd no more found himself in strange trouble at times about his hammock or his clothes bag or what not. As to that smile that occasionally sunned him, and the pleasant passing word, these were, if not more frequent, yet if anything more pronounced than before.

But for all that, there were certain other demonstrations now. When Claggart's unobserved glance happened to light on belted Billy rolling along the upper gun deck in the leisure of the second dog-watch, exchanging passing broadsides of fun with other young promenaders in the crowd, that glance would follow the cheerful sea Hyperion with a settled meditative and melancholy expression, his eyes strangely suffused with incipient feverish tears. Then would Claggart look like the man of sorrows. Yes, and sometimes the melancholy expression would have in it a touch of soft yearning, as if Claggart could even have loved Billy but for fate and ban. But this was an evanescence, and quickly repented of, as it were, by an immitigable look, pinching and shrivelling the visage into the momentary semblance of a wrinkled walnut. But sometimes catching sight in advance of the foretopman coming in his direction, he would, upon their nearing, step aside a little to let him pass, dwelling upon Billy for the moment with the glittering dental satire of a Guise. But upon any abrupt unforeseen encounter a red light would flash forth from his eye like a spark from an anvil in a dusk smithy. That quick, fierce light was a strange one, darted from orbs which in repose were of a color nearest approaching a deeper violet, the softest of shades.

Though some of these caprices of the pit could not but be observed by their object, yet were they beyond the construing of such a nature. And the thews of Billy were hardly compatible with that sort of sensitive spiritual organization which in some cases instinctively conveys to ignorant innocence an admonition of the proximity of the malign. He thought the master-at-arms acted in a manner rather queer at times. That was all. But the occasional frank air and pleasant word went for what they purported to be, the young sailor never having heard as yet of the "too fair-spoken man."

Had the foretopman been conscious of having done or said anything to provoke the ill will of the official, it would have been different with him, and his sight might have been purged if not sharpened. As it was, innocence was his blinder.

So was it with him in yet another matter. Two minor officers, the armorer and captain of the hold, with whom he had never exchanged a word, his position in the ship not bringing him into contact with them, these men now for the first began to cast upon Billy when they chanced to encounter him, that peculiar glance which evidences that the man from whom it comes has been some way tampered with, and to the prejudice of him upon whom the glance lights. Never did it occur to Billy as a thing to be noted or a thing suspicious, though he well knew the fact, that the armorer and captain of the hold, with the ship's yeoman, apothecary, and others of that grade, were by naval usage messmates of the master-at-arms, men with ears convenient to his confidential tongue.

But the general popularity that our Handsome Sailor's manly forwardness bred upon occasion and his irresistible good nature, indicating no mental superiority tending to excite an invidious feeling, this good will on the part of most of his shipmates made him the less to concern himself about such mute aspects toward him as those whereto allusion has just been made, aspects he could not fathom as to infer their whole import.

As to the afterguardsman, though Billy for reasons already given necessarily saw little of him, yet when the two did happen to meet, invariably came the fellow's offhand cheerful recognition, sometimes accompanied by a passing pleasant word or two. Whatever that equivocal young person's original design may really have been, or the design of which he might have been the deputy, certain it was from his manner upon these occasions that he had wholly dropped it.

It was as if his precocity of crookedness (and every vulgar villain is precocious) had for once deceived him, and the man he had sought to entrap as a simpleton had through his very simplicity ignominiously baffled him.

But shrewd ones may opine that it was hardly possible for Billy to refrain from going up to the afterguardsman and bluntly demanding to know his purpose in the initial interview so abruptly closed in the forechains. Shrewd ones may also think it but natural in Billy to set about sounding some of the other impressed men of the ship in order to discover what basis, if any, there was for the emissary's obscure suggestions as to plotting disaffection aboard. Yes, the shrewd may so think. But something more, or rather something else than mere shrewdness is perhaps needful for the due understanding of such a character as Billy Budd's.

As to Claggart, the monomania in the man—if that indeed it were— as involuntarily disclosed by starts in the manifestations detailed, yet in general covered over by his self-contained and rational demeanor; this, like a subterranean fire, was eating its way deeper and deeper in him. Something decisive must come of it.

18

After the mysterious interview in the forechains, the one so abruptly ended there by Billy, nothing especially german to the story occurred until the events now about to be narrated.

Elsewhere it has been said that in the lack of frigates (of course better sailers than line-of-battle ships) in the English squadron up the Straits at that period, the *Bellipotent* was occasionally employed not only as an avail-

able substitute for a scout, but at times on detached service of more important kind. This was not alone because of her sailing qualities, not common
in a ship of her rate, but quite as much, probably, that the character of her
commander, it was thought, specially adapted him for any duty where under unforeseen difficulties a prompt initiative might have to be taken in
some matter demanding knowledge and ability in addition to those qualities implied in good seamanship. It was on an expedition of the latter sort,
a somewhat distant one, and when the *Bellipotent* was almost at her furthest
remove from the fleet, that in the latter part of an afternoon-watch she
unexpectedly came in sight of a ship of the enemy. It proved to be a frigate.
The latter perceiving through the glass that the weight of men and metal
would be heavily against her, invoking her light heels, crowded sail to get
away. After a chase urged almost against hope and lasting until about the
middle of the first dog-watch, she signally succeeded in effecting her escape.

Not long after the pursuit had been given up, and ere the excitement
incident thereto had altogether waned away, the master-at-arms, ascending
from his cavernous sphere, made his appearance cap in hand by the mainmast, respectfully waiting the notice of Captain Vere then solitary walking
the weather side of the quarter-deck, doubtless somewhat chafed at the
failure of the pursuit. The spot where Claggart stood was the place allotted
to men of lesser grades seeking some more particular interview either with
the officer of the deck or the Captain himself. But from the latter it was not
often that a sailor or petty officer of those days would seek a hearing; only
some exceptional cause would, according to established custom, have warranted that.

Presently, just as the commander, absorbed in his reflections, was on
the point of turning aft in his promenade, he became sensible of Claggart's
presence, and saw the doffed cap held in deferential expectancy. Here be it
said that Captain Vere's personal knowledge of this petty officer had only
begun at the time of the ship's last sailing from home, Claggart then for the
first, in transfer from a ship detained for repairs, supplying on board the
Bellipotent the place of a previous master-at-arms disabled and ashore.

No sooner did the commander observe who it was that deferentially
stood awaiting his notice, than a peculiar expression came over him. It was
not unlike that which uncontrollably will flit across the countenance of one
at unawares encountering a person who, though known to him indeed, has
hardly been long enough known for thorough knowledge, but something

in whose aspect nevertheless now for the first provokes a vaguely repellent distaste. But coming to a stand, and resuming much of his wonted official manner, save that a sort of impatience lurked in the intonation of the opening word, he said, "Well? What is it, master-at-arms?"

With the air of a subordinate grieved at the necessity of being a messenger of ill tidings, and while conscientiously determined to be frank, yet equally resolved upon shunning overstatement, Claggart, at this invitation or rather summons to disburthen, spoke up. What he said, conveyed in the language of no uneducated man, was to the effect following, if not altogether in these words, namely, that during the chase and preparations for the possible encounter he had seen enough to convince him that at least one sailor aboard was a dangerous character in a ship mustering some who not only had taken a guilty part in the late serious troubles, but others also who, like the man in question, had entered His Majesty's service under another form than enlistment.

At this point Captain Vere with some impatience interrupted him: "Be direct, man; say *impressed men.*"

Claggart made a gesture of subservience, and proceeded. Quite lately he (Claggart) had begun to suspect that on the gun decks some sort of movement prompted by the sailor in question was covertly going on, but he had not thought himself warranted in reporting the suspicion so long as it remained indistinct. But from what he had that afternoon observed in the man referred to, the suspicion of something clandestine going on had advanced to a point less removed from certainty. He deeply felt, he added, the serious responsibility assumed in making a report involving such possible consequences to the individual mainly concerned, besides tending to augment those natural anxieties which every naval commander must feel in view of extraordinary outbreaks so recent as those which, he sorrowfully said it, it needed not to name.

Now at the first broaching of the matter Captain Vere, taken by surprise, could not wholly dissemble his disquietude. But as Claggart went on, the former's aspect changed into restiveness under something in the witness' manner in giving his testimony. However, he refrained from interrupting him. And Claggart, continuing, concluded with this: "God forbid, your honor, that the *Bellipotent*'s should be the experience of the——"

"Never mind that!" here peremptorily broke in the superior, his face altering with anger, instinctively divining the ship that the other was about to name, one in which the Nore Mutiny had assumed a singularly tragical character that for a time jeopardized the life of its commander. Under the circumstances he was indignant at the purposed allusion. When the commissioned officers themselves were on all occasions very heedful how they referred to the recent events, for a petty officer unnecessarily to allude to them in the presence of his captain, this struck him as a most immodest presumption. Besides, to his quick sense of self-respect, it even looked under the circumstances something like an attempt to alarm him. Nor at first was he without some surprise that one who so far as he had hitherto come under his notice had shown considerable tact in his function should in this particular evince such lack of it.

But these thoughts and kindred dubious ones flitting across his mind were suddenly replaced by an intuitional surmise which, though as yet obscure in form, served practically to affect his reception of the ill tidings. Certain it is, that long versed in everything pertaining to the complicated gun-deck life, which like every other form of life, has its secret mines and dubious side, the side popularly disclaimed, Captain Vere did not permit himself to be unduly disturbed by the general tenor of his subordinate's report.

Furthermore, if in view of recent events prompt action should be taken at the first palpable sign of recurring insubordination, for all that, not judicious would it be, he thought, to keep the idea of lingering disaffection alive by undue forwardness in crediting an informer, even if his own subordinate, and charged among other things with police surveillance of the crew. This feeling would not perhaps have so prevailed with him were it not that upon a prior occasion the patriotic zeal officially evinced by Claggart had somewhat irritated him as appearing rather supersensible and strained. Furthermore, something even in the official's self-possessed and somewhat ostentatious manner in making his specifications strangely reminded him of a bandsman, a perjurous witness in a capital case before a courtmartial ashore of which when a lieutenant he (Captain Vere) had been a member.

Now the peremptory check given to Claggart in the matter of the arrested allusion was quickly followed up by this: "You say that there is at least one dangerous man aboard. Name him."

"William Budd, a foretopman, your honor."

"William Budd!" repeated Captain Vere with unfeigned astonishment. "And mean you the man that Lieutenant Ratcliff took from the merchantman not very long ago, the young fellow who seems to be so popular with the men—Billy, the Handsome Sailor, as they call him?"

"The same, your honor; but for all his youth and good looks, a deep one. Not for nothing does he insinuate himself into the good will of his shipmates, since at the least they will at a pinch say—all hands will—a good word for him, and at all hazards. Did Lieutenant Ratcliff happen to tell your honor of that adroit fling of Budd's, jumping up in the cutter's bow under the merchantman's stern when he was being taken off? It is even masqued by that sort of good-humoured air that at heart he resents his impressment. You have but noted his fair cheek. A mantrap may be under his ruddy-tipped daisies."

Now the Handsome Sailor as a signal figure among the crew had naturally enough attracted the captain's attention from the first. Though in general not very demonstrative to his officers, he had congratulated Lieutenant Ratcliff upon his good fortune in lighting on such a fine specimen of the *genus homo*, who in the nude might have posed for a statue of young Adam before the Fall. As to Billy's adieu to the ship *Rights-of-Man*, which the boarding lieutenant had indeed reported to him, but in a deferential way more as a good story than aught else, Captain Vere, though mistakenly understanding it as a satiric sally, had but thought so much the better of the impressed man for it; as a military sailor, admiring the spirit that could take an arbitrary enlistment so merrily and sensibly. The foretopman's conduct, too, so far as it had fallen under the captain's notice, had confirmed the first happy augury, while the new recruit's qualities as a "sailor-man" seemed to be such that he had thought of recommending him to the executive officer for promotion to a place that would more frequently bring him under his own observation, namely, the captaincy of the mizzentop, replacing there in the starboard watch a man not so young whom partly for that reason he deemed less fitted for the post. Be it parenthesized here that since the mizzentopmen having not to handle such breadths of heavy canvas as the lower sails on the main mast and fore mast, a young man if of the right stuff not only seems best adapted to duty there, but in fact is generally selected for the captaincy of that top, and the company under him are light hands and often but striplings. In sum, Captain Vere had from the beginning deemed Billy Budd to be what in the naval parlance of the time was called a "King's bargain": that is to say, for His Britannic Majesty's Navy a capital investment at small outlay or none at all.

After a brief pause, during which the reminiscences above mentioned passed vividly through his mind and he weighed the import of Claggart's last suggestion conveyed in the phrase "mantrap under his daisies," and the more he weighed it the less reliance he felt in the informer's good faith, suddenly he turned upon him and in a low voice: "Do you come to me, Master-at-arms, with so foggy a tale? As to Budd, cite me an act or spoken word of his confirmatory of what you in general charge against him. Stay," drawing nearer to him, "heed what you speak. Just now, and in a case like this, there is a yard-arm-end for the false-witness."

"Ah, your honor!" sighed Claggart, mildly shaking his shapely head as in sad deprecation of such unmerited severity of tone. Then, bridling—erecting himself as in virtuous self-assertion—he circumstantially alleged certain words and acts, which collectively, if credited, led to presumptions mortally inculpating Budd. And for some of these averments, he added, substantiating proof was not far.

With gray eyes impatient and distrustful essaying to fathom to the bottom Claggart's calm violet ones, Captain Vere again heard him out; then for the moment stood ruminating. The mood he evinced, Claggart—himself for the time liberated from the other's scrutiny—steadily regarded with a look difficult to render,—a look curious of the operation of his tactics, a look such as might have been that of the spokesman of the envious children of Jacob deceptively imposing upon the troubled patriarch the blood-dyed coat of young Joseph.

Though something exceptional in the moral quality of Captain Vere made him, in earnest encounter with a fellow-man, a veritable touch-stone of that man's essential nature, yet now as to Claggart and what was really going on in him, his feeling partook less of intuitional conviction than of strong suspicion clogged by strange dubieties. The perplexity he evinced proceeded less from aught touching the man informed against—as Claggart doubtless opined—than from considerations how best to act in regard to the informer. At first indeed he was naturally for summoning that substantiation of his allegations which Claggart said was at hand. But such a proceeding would result in the matter at once getting abroad, which in the present stage of it, he thought, might undesirably affect the ship's company. If Claggart was a false witness—that closed the affair. And therefore before trying the accusation, he would first practically test the accuser; and he thought this could be done in a quiet undemonstrative way.

The measure he determined upon involved a shifting of the scene, a transfer to a place less exposed to observation than the broad quarter-deck. For although the few gun-room officers there at the time had, in due observance of naval etiquette, withdrawn to leeward the moment Captain Vere had begun his promenade on the deck's weather side; and though during the colloquy with Claggart they of course ventured not to diminish the distance; and though throughout the interview Captain Vere's voice was far from high, and Claggart's silvery and low; and the wind in the cordage and the wash of the sea helped the more to put them beyond earshot; nevertheless, the interview's continuance already had attracted observation from some topmen aloft and other sailors in the waist or further forward.

Having determined upon his measures, Captain Vere forthwith took action. Abruptly turning to Claggart he asked, "Master-at-arms, is it now Budd's watch aloft?"

"No, your honor."

Whereupon, "Mr. Wilkes!" summoning the nearest midshipman. "Tell Albert to come to me." Albert was the captain's hammock-boy, a sort of sea valet in whose discretion and fidelity his master had much confidence. The lad appeared.

"You know Budd, the foretopman?"

"I do, sir."

"Go find him. It is his watch off. Manage to tell him out of earshot that he is wanted aft. Contrive it that he speaks to nobody. Keep him in talk yourself. And not till you get well aft here, not till then let him know that the place where he is wanted is my cabin. You understand. Go.—Master-at-arms, show yourself on the decks below, and when you think it time for Albert to be coming with his man, stand by quietly to follow the sailor in."

19

Now when the foretopman found himself in the cabin, closeted there, as it were, with the captain and Claggart, he was surprised enough. But it was a surprise unaccompanied by apprehension or distrust. To an immature nature essentially honest and humane, forewarning intimations of subtler danger from one's kind come tardily if at all. The only thing that took shape in the young sailor's mind was this: Yes, the captain, I have always thought, looks kindly upon me. Wonder if he's going to make me his coxswain. I should like that. And maybe now he is going to ask the master-at-arms about me.

"Shut the door there, sentry," said the commander; "stand without, and let nobody come in.—Now, Master-at-arms, tell this man to his face what you told of him to me," and stood prepared to scrutinize the mutually confronting visages.

With the measured step and calm collected air of an asylum physician approaching in the public hall some patient beginning to show indications of a coming paroxysm, Claggart deliberately advanced within short range of Billy and, mesmerically looking him in the eye, briefly recapitulated the accusation.

Not at first did Billy take it in. When he did, the rose-tan of his cheek looked struck as by white leprosy. He stood like one impaled and gagged. Meanwhile the accuser's eyes removing not as yet from the blue dilated ones, underwent a phenomenal change, their wonted rich violet color blurring into a muddy purple. Those lights of human intelligence losing human expression, gelidly protruding like the alien eyes of certain uncatalogued creatures of the deep. The first mesmeric glance was one of serpent fascination; the last was as the hungry lurch of the torpedo fish.

"Speak, man!" said Captain Vere to the transfixed one, struck by his aspect even more than by Claggart's, "Speak! defend yourself!" Which appeal caused but a strange dumb gesturing and gurgling in Billy; amazement at such an accusation so suddenly sprung on inexperienced nonage; this, and, it may be, horror of the accuser, serving to bring out his lurking defect and in this instance for the time intensifying it into a convulsed tongue-tie; while the intent head and entire form straining forward in an agony of ineffectual eagerness to obey the injunction to speak and defend himself, gave an expression to the face like that of a condemned Vestal priestess in the moment of being buried alive, and in the first struggle against suffocation.

Though at the time Captain Vere was quite ignorant of Billy's liability to vocal impediment, he now immediately divined it, since vividly Billy's aspect recalled to him that of a bright young schoolmate of his whom he had once seen struck by much the same startling impotence in the act of eagerly rising in the class to be foremost in response to a testing question put to it by the master. Going close up to the young sailor, and laying a soothing hand on his shoulder, he said, "There is no hurry, my boy. Take your time, take your time." Contrary to the effect intended, these words so fatherly in tone, doubtless touching Billy's heart to the quick, prompted yet more violent efforts at utterance—efforts soon ending for the time in confirming the paralysis, and bringing to his face an expression which was as a crucifixion to behold. The next instant, quick as the flame from a discharged cannon at night, his right arm shot out, and Claggart dropped to the deck. Whether intentionally or but owing to the young athlete's superior height, the blow had taken effect fully upon the forehead, so shapely and intellectual-looking a feature in the master-at-arms; so that the body fell over lengthwise, like a heavy plank tilted from erectness. A gasp or two, and he lay motionless.

"Fated boy," breathed Captain Vere in tone so low as to be almost a whisper, "what have you done! But here, help me."

The twain raised the felled one from the loins up into a sitting position. The spare form flexibly acquiesced, but inertly. It was like handling a dead snake. They lowered it back. Regaining erectness Captain Vere with one hand covering his face stood to all appearance as impassive as the object at his feet. Was he absorbed in taking in all the bearings of the event and what was best not only now at once to be done, but also in the sequel? Slowly he uncovered his face; and the effect was as if the moon emerging from eclipse should reappear with quite another aspect than that which had gone into hiding. The father in him, manifested towards Billy thus far in the scene, was replaced by the military disciplinarian. In his official tone he bade the foretopman retire to a state-room aft (pointing it out), and there remain till thence summoned. This order Billy in silence mechanically obeyed. Then going to the cabin-door where it opened on the quarter-deck, Captain Vere said to the sentry without, "Tell somebody to send Albert here." When the lad appeared his master so contrived it that he should not catch sight of the prone one. "Albert," he said to him, "tell the surgeon I wish to see him. You need not come back till called."

When the surgeon entered—a self-poised character of that grave sense and experience that hardly anything could take him aback—Captain Vere advanced to meet him, thus unconsciously intercepting his view of Claggart, and interrupting the other's wonted ceremonious salutation, said, "Nay. Tell me how it is with yonder man," directing his attention to the prostrate one.

The surgeon looked, and for all his self-command, somewhat started at the abrupt revelation. On Claggart's always pallid complexion, thick black blood was now oozing from nostril and ear. To the gazer's professional eye it was unmistakably no living man that he saw.

"Is it so then?" said Captain Vere intently watching him. "I thought it. But verify it." Whereupon the customary tests confirmed the surgeon's first glance, who now looking up in unfeigned concern, cast a look of intense inquisitiveness upon his superior. But Captain Vere, with one hand to his brow, was standing motionless. Suddenly, catching the surgeon's arm convulsively, he exclaimed, pointing down to the body—"It is the divine judgement on Ananias! Look!"

Disturbed by the excited manner he had never before observed in the *Bellipotent*'s captain, and as yet wholly ignorant of the affair, the prudent surgeon nevertheless held his peace, only again looking an earnest interrogation as to what it was that had resulted in such a tragedy.

But Captain Vere was now again motionless standing absorbed in thought. But again starting, he vehemently exclaimed—"Struck dead by an angel of God! Yet the angel must hang!"

At these passionate interjections, mere incoherences to the listener as yet unapprised of the antecedents, the surgeon was profoundly discomposed. But now as recollecting himself, Captain Vere in less passionate tone briefly related the circumstances leading up to the event. "But come; we must despatch," he added. "me to remove him" (meaning the body) "to yonder compartment," designating one opposite that where the foretopman remained immured. Anew disturbed by a request that as implying a desire for secrecy, seemed unaccountably strange to him, there was nothing for the subordinate to do but comply.

"Go now," said Captain Vere with something of his wonted manner. "Go now. I shall presently call a drumhead court. Tell the lieutenants what has happened, and tell Mr. Mordant" (meaning the captain of marines), "and charge them to keep the matter to themselves."

20

Full of disquietude and misgiving the surgeon left the cabin. Was Captain Vere suddenly affected in his mind, or was it but a transient excitement, brought about by so strange and extraordinary a happening? As to the drum-head court, it struck the surgeon as impolitic, if nothing more. The thing to do, he thought, was to place Billy Budd in confinement and in a way dictated by usage, and postpone further action in so extraordinary a case to such time as they should rejoin the squadron, and then refer it to the Admiral. He recalled the unwonted agitation of Captain Vere and his excited exclamations so at variance with his normal manner. Was he unhinged?

But assuming that he is, it is not so susceptible of proof. What then can he do? No more trying situation is conceivable than that of an officer subordinate under a captain whom he suspects to be not mad, indeed, but yet not quite unaffected in his intellects. To argue his order to him would be insolence. To resist him would be mutiny.

In obedience to Captain Vere, he communicated what had happened to the lieutenants and captain of marines, saying nothing as to the captain's state. They fully shared his own surprise and concern. Like him too, they seemed to think that such a matter should be referred to the admiral.

21

Who in the rainbow can draw the line where the violet tint ends and the orange tint begins? Distinctly we see the difference of the colors, but where exactly does the one first blendingly enter into the other? So with sanity and insanity. In pronounced cases there is no question about them. But in some supposed cases, in various degrees supposedly less pronounced, to draw the exact line of demarcation few will undertake though for a fee some professional experts will. There is nothing namable but that some men will undertake to do it for pay.

Whether Captain Vere, as the surgeon professionally and privately surmised, was really the sudden victim of any degree of aberration, one must determine for himself by such light as this narrative may afford.

That the unhappy event which has been narrated could not have happened at a worse juncture was but too true. For it was close on the heel of the suppressed insurrections, an aftertime very critical to naval authority, demanding from every English sea-commander two qualities not readily interfusable—prudence and rigour. Moreover there was something crucial in the case.

In the jugglery of circumstances preceding and attending the event on board the *Bellipotent*, and in the light of that martial code whereby it was formally to be judged, innocence and guilt personified in Claggart and Budd in effect changed places. In a legal view the apparent victim of the tragedy was he who had sought to victimize a man blameless; and the indisputable deed of the latter, navally regarded, constituted the most heinous of military crimes. Yet more. The essential right and wrong involved in the matter, the clearer that might be, so much the worse for the responsibility of a loyal sea-commander inasmuch as he was not authorized to determine the matter on that primitive basis.

Small wonder then that the *Bellipotent*'s captain, though in general a man of rapid decision, felt that circumspectness not less than promptitude was necessary. Until he could decide upon his course, and in each detail; and not only so, but until the concluding measure was upon the point of being enacted, he deemed it advisable, in view of all the circumstances, to guard as much as possible against publicity. Here he may or may not have erred. Certain it is, however, that subsequently in the confidential talk of more than one or two gun rooms and cabins he was not a little criticized by some officers, a fact imputed by his friends and vehemently by his cousin Jack Denton to professional jealousy of Starry Vere. Some imaginative ground for invidious comment there was. The maintenance of secrecy in the matter, the confining all knowledge of it for a time to the place where the homicide occurred, the quarter deck cabin; in these particulars lurked some resemblance to the policy adopted in those tragedies of the palace which have occurred more than once in the capital founded by Peter the Barbarian.

The case indeed was such that fain would the *Bellipotent*'s captain have deferred taking any action whatever respecting it further than to keep the foretopman a close prisoner till the ship rejoined the squadron, and then submitting the matter to the judgement of his Admiral.

But a true military officer is in one particular like a true monk. Not with more of self-abnegation will the latter keep his vows of monastic obedience than the former his vows of allegiance to martial duty.

Feeling that unless quick action was taken on it, the deed of the foretopman, so soon as it should be known on the gun decks, would tend to awaken any slumbering embers of the Nore among the crew, a sense of the urgency of the case overruled in Captain Vere every other consideration. But though a conscientious disciplinarian, he was no lover of authority for mere authority's sake. Very far was he from embracing opportunities for monopolizing to himself the perils of moral responsibility, none at least that could properly be referred to an official superior, or shared with him by his official equals or even subordinates. So thinking, he was glad it would not be at variance with usage to turn the matter over to a summary court of his own officers, reserving to himself as the one on whom the ultimate accountability would rest, the right of maintaining a supervision of it, or formally or informally interposing at need. Accordingly a drum-head court was summarily convened, he electing the individuals composing it, the First Lieutenant, the captain of Marines, and the Sailing Master.

In associating an officer of marines with the sea lieutenant in a case having to do with a sailor, the commander perhaps deviated from general custom. He was prompted thereto by the circumstance that he took that soldier to be a judicious person, thoughtful, and not altogether incapable of grappling with a difficult case unprecedented in his prior experience. Yet even as to him he was not without some latent misgiving, for withal he was an extremely good-natured man, an enjoyer of his dinner, a sound sleeper, and inclined to obesity—a man who though he would always maintain his manhood in battle might not prove altogether reliable in a moral dilemma involving aught of the tragic. As to the first lieutenant and the sailing master, Captain Vere could not but be aware that though honest natures, of approved gallantry upon occasion, their intelligence was mostly confined to the matter of active seamanship and the fighting demands of their profession.

The court was held in the same cabin where the unfortunate affair had taken place. This cabin, the commander's, embraced the entire area under the poopdeck. Aft, and on either side, was a small stateroom; the one room temporarily a jail and the other a dead-house, and a yet smaller compartment leaving a space between, expanding forward into a goodly oblong of length coinciding with the ship's beam. A skylight of moderate dimension was overhead and at each end of the oblong space were two sashed porthole windows easily convertible back into embrasures for short carronades.

All being quickly in readiness, Billy Budd was arraigned, Captain Vere necessarily appearing as the sole witness in the case, and as such temporarily sinking his rank, though singularly maintaining it in a matter apparently trivial, namely, that he testified from the ship's weather side, with that object having caused the court to sit on the lee side. Concisely he narrated all that had led up to the catastrophe, omitting nothing in Claggart's accusation and deposing as to the manner in which the prisoner had received it. At this testimony the three officers glanced with no little surprise at Billy Budd, the last man they would have suspected either of the mutinous design alleged by Claggart or the undeniable deed he himself had done. The first lieutenant, taking judicial primacy and turning toward the prisoner, said, "Captain Vere has spoken. Is it or is it not as Captain Vere says?"

In response came syllables not so much impeded in the utterance as might have been anticipated. They were these: "Captain Vere tells the truth. It is just as Captain Vere says, but it is not as the master-at-arms said. I have eaten the King's bread and I am true to the King."

"I believe you, my man," said the witness, his voice indicating a suppressed emotion not otherwise betrayed.

"God will bless you for that, your honor!" not without stammering said Billy, and all but broke down. But immediately was recalled to self-control by another question, to which with the same emotional difficulty of utterance he said, "No, there was no malice between us. I never bore malice against the master-at-arms. I am sorry that he is dead. I did not mean to kill him. Could I have used my tongue I would not have struck him. But he foully lied to my face and in presence of my captain, and I had to say something, and I could only say it with a blow, God help me!"

In the impulsive above-board manner of the frank one, the court saw confirmed all that was implied in words that just previously had perplexed them, coming as they did from the testifier to the tragedy and promptly following Billy's impassioned disclaimer of mutinous intent—Captain Vere's words, "I believe you, my man."

Next it was asked of him whether he knew of or suspected aught savoring of incipient trouble (meaning mutiny, though the explicit term was avoided) going on in any section of the ship's company.

The reply lingered. This was naturally imputed by the court to the same vocal embarrassment which had retarded or obstructed previous answers. But in main it was otherwise here; the question immediately recalling to Billy's mind the interview with the afterguardsman in the fore-chains. But an innate repugnance to playing a part at all approaching that of an informer against one's own shipmates—the same erring sense of uninstructed honor which had stood in the way of his reporting the matter at the time though as a loyal man-of-war-man it was incumbent on him, and failure so to do if charged against him and proven, would have subjected him to the heaviest of penalties; this, with the blind feeling now his, that nothing really was being hatched, prevailed with him. When the answer came it was a negative.

"One question more," said the officer of marines now first speaking and with a troubled earnestness. "You tell us that what the master-at-arms said against you was a lie. Now why should he have so lied, so maliciously lied, since you declare there was no malice between you?"

At that question, unintentionally touching on a spiritual sphere wholly obscure to Billy's thoughts, he was nonplussed, evincing a confusion indeed that some observers, such as can readily be imagined, would have construed into involuntary evidence of hidden guilt. Nevertheless he strove some way to answer, but all at once relinquished the vain endeavor, at the same time turning an appealing glance towards Captain Vere as deeming him his best helper and friend. Captain Vere, who had been seated for a time, rose to his feet, addressing the interrogator. "The question you put to him comes naturally enough. But how can he rightly answer it?—or anybody else, unless indeed it be he who lies within there," designating the compartment where lay the corpse. "But the prone one there will not rise to our summons. In effect, though, as it seems to me, the point you make is hardly material. Quite aside from any conceivable motive actuating the master-at-arms, and irrespective of the provocation to the blow, a martial court must needs in the present case confine its attention to the blow's consequence, which consequence justly is to be deemed not otherwise than as the striker's deed."

This utterance, the full significance of which it was not at all likely that Billy took in, nevertheless caused him to turn a wistful interrogative look toward the speaker, a look in its dumb expressiveness not unlike that which a dog of generous breed might turn upon his master seeking in his face some elucidation of a previous gesture ambiguous to the canine intelligence. Nor was the same utterance without marked effect upon the three officers, more especially the soldier. Couched in it seemed to them a meaning unanticipated, involving a prejudgement on the speaker's part. It served to augment a mental disturbance previously evident enough.

The soldier once more spoke; in a tone of suggestive dubiety addressing at once his associates and Captain Vere: "Nobody is present—none of the ship's company, I mean—who might shed lateral light, if any is to be had, upon what remains mysterious in this matter."

"That is thoughtfully put," said Captain Vere; "I see your drift. Ay, there is a mystery; but, to use a scriptural phrase, it is 'a mystery of iniquity,' a matter for psychologic theologians to discuss. But what has a military court to do with it? Not to add that for us any possible investigation of it is cut off by the lasting tongue-tie of—him—in yonder," again designating the mortuary stateroom. "The prisoner's deed—with that alone we have to do."

To this, and particularly the closing reiteration, the marine soldier knowing not how aptly to reply, sadly abstained from saying aught. The First Lieutenant who at the outset had not unnaturally assumed primacy in the court, now overrulingly instructed by a glance from Captain Vere, a glance more effective than words, resumed that primacy. Turning to the prisoner, "Budd," he said, and scarce in equable tones, "Budd, if you have aught further to say for yourself, say it now."

Upon this the young sailor turned another quick glance toward Captain Vere; then, as taking a hint from that aspect, a hint confirming his own instinct that silence was now best, replied to the Lieutenant, "I have said all, sir."

The marine—the same who had been the sentinel without the cabin-door at the time that the foretopman followed by the master-at-arms, entered it—he, standing by the sailor throughout these judicial proceedings, was now directed to take him back to the after compartment originally assigned to the prisoner and his custodian. As the twain disappeared from view, the three officers as partially liberated from some inward constraint associated with Billy's mere presence, simultaneously stirred in their seats. They exchanged looks of troubled indecision, yet feeling that decide they must and without long delay. As for Captain Vere, he for the time stood unconsciously with his back toward them, apparently in one of his absent fits, gazing out from a sashed port-hole to windward upon the monotonous blank of the twilight sea. But the court's silence continuing, broken only at moments by brief consultations in low earnest tones, this seemed to arm him and energize him. Turning, he to-and-fro paced the cabin athwart; in the returning ascent to windward, climbing the slant deck in the ship's lee roll; without knowing it symbolizing thus in his action a mind resolute to surmount difficulties even if against primitive instincts strong as the wind and the sea. Presently he came to a stand before the three. After scanning their faces he stood less as mustering his thoughts for expression, than as one inly deliberating how best to put them to well-meaning men not intellectually mature, men with whom it was necessary to demonstrate certain principles that were axioms to himself. Similar impatience as to talking is perhaps one reason that deters some minds from addressing any popular assemblies.

When speak he did, something both in the substance of what he said and his manner of saying it, showed the influence of unshared studies modifying and tempering the practical training of an active career. This, along with his phraseology, now and then was suggestive of the grounds whereon rested that imputation of a certain pedantry socially alleged against him by certain naval men of wholly practical cast, captains who nevertheless would frankly concede that His Majesty's Navy mustered no more efficient officer of their grade than Starry Vere.

What he said was to this effect: "Hitherto I have been but the witness, little more; and I should hardly think now to take another tone, that of your coadjutor, for the time, did I not perceive in you—at the crisis too—a troubled hesitancy, proceeding, I doubt not, from the clash of military duty with moral scruple—scruple vitalized by compassion. For the compassion, how can I otherwise than share it? But, mindful of paramount obligations I strive against scruples that may tend to enervate decision. Not, gentlemen, that I hide from myself that the case is an exceptional one. Speculatively regarded, it well might be referred to a jury of casuists. But for us here acting not as casuists or moralists, it is a case practical, and under martial law practically to be dealt with.

"But your scruples: do they move as in a dusk? Challenge them. Make them advance and declare themselves. Come now: do they import something like this? If, mindless of palliating circumstances, we are bound to regard the death of the master-at-arms as the prisoner's deed, then does that deed constitute a capital crime whereof the penalty is a mortal one? But in natural justice is nothing but the prisoner's overt act to be considered? How can we adjudge to summary and shameful death a fellow-creature innocent before God, and whom we feel to be so?—Does that state it aright? You sign sad assent. Well, I too feel that, the full force of that. It is Nature. But do these buttons that we wear attest that our allegiance is to Nature? No, to the King. Though the ocean, which is inviolate Nature primeval, though this be the element where we move and have our being as sailors, yet as the King's officers lies our duty in a sphere correspondingly natural? So little is that true, that in receiving our commissions we in the most important regards ceased to be natural free agents. When war is declared are we the commissioned fighters previously consulted? We fight at command. If our judgements approve the war, that is but coincidence. So in other particulars. So now. For suppose condemnation to follow these present proceedings. Would it be so much we ourselves that would condemn as it would be martial law operating through us? For that law and the rigor of it, we are not responsible. Our avowed responsibility is in this: That however pitilessly that law may operate, we nevertheless adhere to it and administer it.

"But the exceptional in the matter moves the hearts within you. Even so too is mine moved. But let not warm hearts betray heads that should be cool. Ashore in a criminal case will an upright judge allow himself off the bench to be waylaid by some tender kinswoman of the accused seeking to touch him with her tearful plea? Well the heart here denotes the feminine in man is as that piteous woman, and hard though it be, she must here be ruled out."

He paused, earnestly studying them for a moment; then resumed.

"But something in your aspect seems to urge that it is not solely the heart that moves in you, but also the conscience, the private conscience. But tell me whether or not, occupying the position we do, private conscience should not yield to that imperial one formulated in the code under which alone we officially proceed?"

Here the three men moved in their seats, less convinced than agitated by the course of an argument troubling but the more the spontaneous conflict within.

Perceiving which, the speaker paused for a moment; then abruptly changing his tone, went on.

"To steady us a bit, let us recur to the facts.—In war-time at sea a man-of-war's-man strikes his superior in grade, and the blow kills. Apart from its effect, the blow itself is, according to the Articles of War, a capital crime. Furthermore—"

"Ay, sir," emotionally broke in the officer of marines, "in one sense it was. But surely Budd purposed neither mutiny nor homicide."

"Surely not, my good man. And before a court less arbitrary and more merciful than a martial one, that plea would largely extenuate. At the Last Assizes it shall acquit. But how here? We proceed under the law of the Mutiny Act. In feature no child can resemble his father more than that Act resembles in spirit the thing from which it derives—War. In His Majesty's service—in this ship, indeed—there are Englishmen forced to fight for the King against their will. Against their conscience, for aught we know. Though as their fellow creatures some of us may appreciate their position, yet as navy officers, what reck we of it? Still less recks the enemy. Our impressed men he would fain cut down in the same swath with our volunteers. As regards the enemy's naval conscripts, some of whom may even share our own abhorrence of the regicidal French Directory, it is the same on our side. War looks but to the frontage, the appearance. And the Mutiny Act,

War's child, takes after the father. Budd's intent or non-intent is nothing to the purpose.

"But while, put to it by these anxieties in you which I can not but respect, I only repeat myself—while thus strangely we prolong proceedings that should be summary—the enemy may be sighted and an engagement result. We must do; and one of two things must we do—condemn or let go."

"Can we not convict and yet mitigate the penalty?" asked the sailing master, here speaking, and falteringly, for the first.

"Gentlemen, were that clearly lawful for us under the circumstances, consider the consequences of such clemency. The people" (meaning the ship's company) "have native sense; most of them are familiar with our naval usage and tradition; and how would they take it? Even could you explain to them—which our official position forbids—they, long moulded by arbitrary discipline have not that kind of intelligent responsiveness that might qualify them to comprehend and discriminate. No, to the people the foretopman's deed, however it be worded in the announcement, will be plain homicide committed in a flagrant act of mutiny. What penalty for that should follow, they know. But it does not follow. *Why?* they will ruminate. You know what sailors are. Will they not revert to the recent outbreak at the Nore? Ay. They know the well-founded alarm—the panic it struck throughout England. Your clement sentence they would account pusillanimous. They would think that we flinch, that we are afraid of them—afraid of practising a lawful rigour singularly demanded at this juncture lest it should provoke new troubles. What shame to us such a conjecture on their part, and how deadly to discipline. You see then, whither, prompted by duty and the law, I steadfastly drive. But I beseech you, my friends, do not take me amiss. I feel as you do for this unfortunate boy. But did he know our hearts, I take him to be of that generous nature that he would feel even for us on whom in this military necessity so heavy a compulsion is laid."

With that, crossing the deck he resumed his place by the sashed port-hole, tacitly leaving the three to come to a decision. On the cabin's opposite side the troubled court sat silent. Loyal lieges, plain and practical, though at bottom they dissented from some points Captain Vere had put to them, they were without the faculty, hardly had the inclination, to gainsay one whom they felt to be an earnest man, one too not less their superior in mind than in naval rank. But it is not improbable that even such of his words as were not without influence over them, less came home to them

131

than his closing appeal to their instinct as sea-officers in the forethought he threw out as to the practical consequences to discipline, considering the unconfirmed tone of the fleet at the time, should a man-of-war's-man's violent killing at sea of a superior in grade be allowed to pass for aught else than a capital crime demanding prompt infliction of the penalty.

Not unlikely they were brought to something more or less akin to that harassed frame of mind which in the year 1842 actuated the commander of the U.S. brig-of-war *Somers* to resolve, under the so-called Articles of War, Articles modelled upon the English Mutiny Act, to resolve upon the execution at sea of a midshipman and two petty officers as mutineers designing the seizure of the brig. Which resolution was carried out though in a time of peace and within not many days' of home. An act vindicated by a naval court of inquiry subsequently convened ashore. History, and here cited without comment. True, the circumstances on board the Somers were different from those on board the *Bellipotent*. But the urgency felt, well-warranted or otherwise, was much the same.

Says a writer whom few know, "Forty years after a battle it is easy for a noncombatant to reason about how it ought to have been fought. It is another thing personally and under fire to direct the fighting while involved in the obscuring smoke of it. Much so with respect to other emergencies involving considerations both practical and moral, and when it is imperative promptly to act. The greater the fog the more it imperils the steamer, and speed is put on though at the hazard of running somebody down. Little ween the snug card-players in the cabin of the responsibilities of the sleepless man on the bridge."

In brief, Billy Budd was formally convicted and sentenced to be hung at the yard-arm in the early morning watch, it being now night. Otherwise, as is customary in such cases, the sentence would forthwith have been carried out. In war-time on the field or in the fleet, a mortal punishment decreed by a drum-head court—on the field sometimes decreed by but a nod from the General—follows without delay on the heel of conviction, without appeal.

22

It was Captain Vere himself who of his own motion communicated the finding of the court to the prisoner; for that purpose going to the compartment where he was in custody and bidding the marine there to withdraw for the time.

Beyond the communication of the sentence what took place at this interview was never known. But in view of the character of the twain briefly closeted in that stateroom, each radically sharing in the rarer qualities of our nature—so rare indeed as to be all but incredible to average minds however much cultivated—some conjectures may be ventured.

It would have been in consonance with the spirit of Captain Vere should he on this occasion have concealed nothing from the condemned one—should he indeed have frankly disclosed to him the part he himself had played in bringing about the decision, at the same time revealing his actuating motives. On Billy's side it is not improbable that such a confession would have been received in much the same spirit that prompted it. Not without a sort of joy indeed he might have appreciated the brave opinion of him implied in his captain's making such a confidant of him. Nor, as to the sentence itself could he have been insensible that it was imparted to him as to one not afraid to die. Even more may have been. Captain Vere in the end may have developed the passion sometimes latent under an exterior stoical or indifferent. He was old enough to have been Billy's father. The austere devotee of military duty, letting himself melt back into what remains primeval in our formalized humanity, may in the end have caught Billy to his heart even as Abraham may have caught young Isaac on the brink of resolutely offering him up in obedience to the exacting behest. But there is no telling the sacrament, seldom if in any case revealed to the gadding world, wherever under circumstances at all akin to those here attempted to be set forth, two of great Nature's nobler order embrace. There is privacy at the time, inviolable to the survivor, and holy oblivion, the sequel to each diviner magnanimity, providentially covers all at last.

The first to encounter Captain Vere in act of leaving the compartment was the senior Lieutenant. The face he beheld, for the moment one expressive of the agony of the strong, was to that officer, though a man of fifty, a startling revelation. That the condemned one suffered less than he who mainly had effected the condemnation was apparently indicated by the former's exclamation in the scene soon perforce to be touched upon.

23

Of a series of incidents within a brief term rapidly following each other, the adequate narration may take up a term less brief, especially if explanation or comment here and there seem requisite to the better understanding of such incidents. Between the entrance into the cabin of him who never left it alive, and him who when he did leave it left it as one condemned to die; between this and the closeted interview just given, less than an hour and a half had elapsed. It was an interval long enough however to awaken speculations among no few of the ship's company as to what it was that could be detaining in the cabin the master-at-arms and the sailor; for a rumor that both of them had been seen to enter it and neither of them had been seen to emerge, this rumor had got abroad upon the gun decks and in the tops; the people of a great war-ship being in one respect like villagers taking microscopic note of every outward movement or non-movement going on. When therefore in weather not at all tempestuous all hands were called in the second dog-watch, a summons under such circumstances not usual in those hours, the crew were not wholly unprepared for some announcement extraordinary, one having connection too with the continued absence of the two men from their wonted haunts.

There was a moderate sea at the time; and the moon, newly risen and near to being at its full, silvered the white spar-deck wherever not blotted by the clear-cut shadows horizontally thrown of fixtures and moving men. On either side of the quarter deck, the marine guard under arms was drawn up; and Captain Vere standing in his place surrounded by all the wardroom officers, addressed his men. In so doing his manner showed neither more nor less than that properly pertaining to his supreme position aboard his own ship. In clear terms and concise he told them what had taken place in the cabin; that the master-at-arms was dead; that he who had killed him had been already tried by a summary court and condemned to death; and that the execution would take place in the early morning watch. The word *mutiny* was not named in what he said. He refrained too from making the occasion an opportunity for any preachment as to the maintenance of discipline, thinking perhaps that under existing circumstances in the navy the consequence of violating discipline should be made to speak for itself.

Their captain's announcement was listened to by the throng of standing sailors in a dumbness like that of a seated congregation of believers in hell listening to the clergyman's announcement of his Calvinistic text.

At the close, however, a confused murmur went up. It began to wax. All but instantly, then, at a sign, it was pierced and suppressed by shrill whistles of the boatswain and his mates piping down one watch. The word was given to about ship.

To be prepared for burial Claggart's body was delivered to certain petty officers of his mess. And here, not to clog the sequel with lateral matters, it may be added that at a suitable hour, the master-at-arms was committed to the sea with every funeral honor properly belonging to his naval grade.

In this proceeding as in every public one growing out of the tragedy, strict adherence to usage was observed. Nor in any point could it have been at all deviated from, either with respect to Claggart or Billy Budd, without begetting undesirable speculations in the ship's company, sailors, and more particularly men-of-war's-men, being of all men the greatest sticklers for usage. For similar cause, all communication between Captain Vere and the condemned one ended with the closeted interview already given, the latter being now surrendered to the ordinary routine preliminary to the end. This transfer under guard from the captain's quarters was effected without un- usual precautions—at least no visible ones. If possible, not to let the men so much as surmise that their officers anticipate aught amiss from them is the tacit rule in a military ship. And the more that some sort of trouble should really be apprehended the more do the officers keep that apprehen- sion to themselves; though not the less unostentatious vigilance may be augmented. In the present instance, the sentry placed over the prisoner had strict orders to let no one have communication with him but the chaplain. And certain unobtrusive measures were taken absolutely to insure this point.

24

In a seventy-four of the old order the deck known as the upper gun deck was the one covered over by the spar-deck which last though not without its armament was for the most part exposed to the weather. In general it was at all hours free from hammocks; those of the crew swinging on the lower gun deck, and berth-deck, the latter being not only a dormi- tory but also the place for the stowing of the sailors' bags, and on both sides lined with the large chests or movable pantries of the many messes of the men.

On the starboard side of the *Bellipotent*'s upper gun deck, behold Billy Budd under sentry, lying prone in irons, in one of the bays formed by the regular spacing of the guns comprising the batteries on either side. All these pieces were of the heavier calibre of that period. Mounted on lumbering wooden carriages they were hampered with cumbersome harness of breechen and strong side-tackles for running them out. Guns and carriages, together with the long rammers and shorter lintstocks lodged in loops overhead—all these, as customary, were painted black; and the heavy hempen breechens, tarred to the same tint, wore the like livery of the undertakers. In contrast with the funereal hue of these surroundings the prone sailor's exterior apparel, white jumper and white duck trousers, each more or less soiled, dimly glimmered in the obscure light of the bay like a patch of discolored snow in early April lingering at some upland cave's black mouth. In effect he is already in his shroud or the garments that shall serve him in lieu of one. Over him, but scarce illuminating him, two battle-lanterns swing from two massive beams of the deck above. Fed with the oil supplied by the war-contractors (whose gains, honest or otherwise, are in every land an anticipated portion of the harvest of death), with flickering splashes of dirty yellow light they pollute the pale moonshine all but ineffectually struggling in obstructed flecks through the open ports from which the tompioned cannon protrude. Other lanterns at intervals serve but to bring out somewhat the obscurer bays which, like small confessionals or side-chapels in a cathedral, branch from the long dim-vistaed broad aisle between the two batteries of that covered tier.

Such was the deck where now lay the Handsome Sailor. Through the rose-tan of his complexion, no pallor could have shown. It would have taken days of sequestration from the winds and the sun to have brought about the effacement of that. But the skeleton in the cheekbone at the point of its angle was just beginning delicately to be defined under the warm-tinted skin. In fervid hearts self-contained, some brief experiences devour our human tissue as secret fire in a ship's hold consumes cotton in the bale.

But now lying between the two guns, as nipped in the vice of fate, Billy's agony, mainly proceeding from a generous young heart's virgin experience of the diabolical incarnate and effective in some men—the tension of that agony was over now. It survived not the something healing in the closeted interview with Captain Vere. Without movement, he lay as in a trance. That adolescent expression previously noted as his, taking on something akin to the look of a slumbering child in the cradle when the warm hearth-glow of the still chamber at night plays on the dimples that at whiles mysteriously form in the cheek, silently coming and going there. For now and then in the gyved one's trance a serene happy light born of some wandering reminiscence or dream would diffuse itself over his face, and then wane away only anew to return.

The chaplain, coming to see him and finding him thus, and perceiving no sign that he was conscious of his presence, attentively regarded him for a space, then slipping aside, withdrew for the time, peradventure feeling that even he the minister of Christ, though receiving his stipend from Mars, had no consolation to proffer which could result in a peace transcending that which he beheld. But in the small hours he came again. And the prisoner, now awake to his surroundings, noticed his approach, and civilly, all but cheerfully, welcomed him. But it was to little purpose that in the interview following the good man sought to bring Billy Budd to some godly understanding that he must die, and at dawn. True, Billy himself freely referred to his death as a thing close at hand; but it was something in the way that children will refer to death in general, who yet among their other sports will play a funeral with hearse and mourners.

Not that like children Billy was incapable of conceiving what death really is. No, but he was wholly without irrational fear of it, a fear more prevalent in highly civilized communities than those so-called barbarous ones which in all respects stand nearer to unadulterate Nature. And, as elsewhere said, a barbarian Billy radically was; as much so, for all the costume, as his countrymen the British captives, living trophies, made to march in the Roman triumph of Germanicus. Quite as much so as those later barbarians, young men probably, and picked specimens among the earlier British converts to Christianity, at least nominally such, and taken to Rome (as to-day converts from lesser isles of the sea may be taken to London), of whom the Pope of that time, admiring the strangeness of their personal beauty so unlike the Italian stamp, their clear ruddy complexion and curled flaxen locks, exclaimed, "Angles" (meaning *English*, the modern derivative) "Angles, do you call them? And is it because they look so like angels?" Had it been later in time one would think that the Pope had in mind Fra Angelico's seraphs some of whom, plucking apples in gardens of the Hesperides, have the faint rose-bud complexion of the more beautiful English girls.

If in vain the good Chaplain sought to impress the young barbarian with ideas of death akin to those conveyed in the skull, dial, and cross-bones on old tombstones; equally futile to all appearance were his efforts to bring home to him the thought of salvation and a Saviour. Billy listened, but less out of awe or reverence perhaps than from a certain natural politeness; doubtless at bottom regarding all that in much the same way that most mariners of his class take any discourse abstract or out of the common tone of the work-a-day world. And this sailor-way of taking clerical discourse is not wholly unlike the way in which the pioneer of Christianity full of transcendent miracles was received long ago on tropic isles by any superior *savage* so called—a Tahitian say of Captain Cook's time or shortly after that time. Out of natural courtesy he received, but did not appropriate. It was like a gift placed in the palm of an outreached hand upon which the fingers do not close.

But the *Bellipotent*'s chaplain was a discreet man possessing the good sense of a good heart. So he insisted not in his vocation here. At the instance of Captain Vere, a lieutenant had apprised him of pretty much everything as to Billy; and since he felt that innocence was even a better thing than religion wherewith to go to Judgement, he reluctantly withdrew; but in his emotion not without first performing an act strange enough in an Englishman, and under the circumstances yet more so in any regular priest. Stooping over, he kissed on the fair cheek his fellow man, a felon in martial law, one who though on the confines of death he felt he could never convert to a dogma; nor for all that did he fear for his future.

Marvel not that having been made acquainted with the young sailor's essential innocence the worthy man lifted not a finger to avert the doom of such a martyr to martial discipline. So to do would not only have been as idle as invoking the desert, but would also have been an audacious transgression of the bounds of his function, one as exactly prescribed to him by military law as that of the boatswain or any other naval officer. Bluntly put, a chaplain is the minister of the Prince of Peace serving in the host of the God of War—Mars. As such, he is as incongruous as a musket would be on the altar at Christmas. Why, then, is he there? Because he indirectly subserves the purpose attested by the cannon; because too he lends the sanction of the religion of the meek to that which practically is the abrogation of everything but brute Force.

25

The night so luminous on the spar deck, but otherwise on the cavernous ones below, levels so like the tiered galleries in a coal mine—the luminous night passed away. But, like the prophet in the chariot disappearing in heaven and dropping his mantle to Elisha, the withdrawing night transferred its pale robe to the breaking day. A meek shy light appeared in the East, where stretched a diaphanous fleece of white furrowed vapor. That light slowly waxed. Suddenly *eight bells* was struck aft, responded to by one louder metallic stroke from forward. It was four o'clock in the morning. Instantly the silver whistles were heard summoning all hands to witness punishment. Up through the great hatchways rimmed with racks of heavy shot, the watch below came pouring, overspreading with the watch already on deck the space between the main mast and fore mast including that occupied by the capacious launch and the black booms tiered on either side of it, boat and booms making a summit of observation for the powderboys and younger tars. A different group comprising one watch of topmen leaned over the rail of that sea balcony, no small one in a seventy-four, looking down on the crowd below. Man or boy, none spake but in whisper, and few spake at all. Captain Vere—as before, the central figure among the assembled commissioned officers—stood nigh the break of the poop deck facing forward. Just below him on the quarter-deck the marines in full equipment were drawn up much as at the scene of the promulgated sentence.

At sea in the old time, the execution by halter of a military sailor was generally from the foreyard. In the present instance, for special reasons the mainyard was assigned. Under an arm of that yard the prisoner was presently brought up, the chaplain attending him. It was noted at the time and remarked upon afterwards, that in this final scene the good man evinced little or nothing of the perfunctory. Brief speech indeed he had with the condemned one, but the genuine Gospel was less on his tongue than in his aspect and manner towards him. The final preparations personal to the latter being speedily brought to an end by two boatswain's mates, the consummation impended. Billy stood facing aft. At the penultimate moment, his words, his only ones, words wholly unobstructed in the utterance were these "God bless Captain Vere!" Syllables so unanticipated coming from one with the ignominious hemp about his neck—a conventional felon's benediction directed aft towards the quarters of honor; syllables too delivered in the clear melody of a singing bird on the point of launching from the twig, had a phenomenal effect, not unenhanced by the rare personal beauty of the young sailor spiritualized now through late experiences so poignantly profound.

Without volition as it were, as if indeed the ship's populace were but the vehicles of some vocal current electric, with one voice from alow and aloft came a resonant sympathetic echo: "God bless Captain Vere!" And yet at that instant Billy alone must have been in their hearts, even as he was in their eyes.

At the pronounced words and the spontaneous echo that voluminously rebounded them, Captain Vere, either through stoic self-control or a sort of momentary paralysis induced by emotional shock, stood erectly rigid as a musket in the ship-armorer's rack.

The hull deliberately recovering from the periodic roll to leeward was just regaining an even keel, when the last signal, a preconcerted dumb one, was given. At the same moment it chanced that the vapory fleece hanging low in the East, was shot through with a soft glory as of the fleece of the Lamb of God seen in mystical vision, and simultaneously therewith, watched by the wedged mass of upturned faces, Billy ascended; and, ascending, took the full rose of the dawn.

In the pinioned figure, arrived at the yard-end, to the wonder of all no motion was apparent, none save that created by the ship's motion, in moderate weather so majestic in a great ship ponderously cannoned.

26

When some days afterwards, in reference to the singularity just mentioned, the purser, a rather ruddy, rotund person more accurate as an accountant than profound as a philosopher, said at mess to the surgeon, "What testimony to the force lodged in will power," the latter, saturnine, spare and tall, one in whom a discreet causticity went along with a manner less genial than polite, replied, "Your pardon, Mr. Purser. In a hanging scientifically conducted—and under special orders I myself directed how Budd's was to be effected—any movement following the completed suspension and originating in the body suspended, such movement indicates mechanical spasm in the muscular system. Hence the absence of that is no more attributable to will-power as you call it than to horse-power—begging your pardon."

"But this muscular spasm you speak of, is not that in a degree more or less invariable in these cases?"

"Assuredly so, Mr. Purser."

"How then, my good sir, do you account for its absence in this instance?"

"Mr. Purser, it is clear that your sense of the singularity in this matter equals not mine. You account for it by what you call will-power—a term not yet included in the lexicon of science. For me I do not, with my present knowledge, pretend to account for it at all. Even should we assume the hypothesis that at the first touch of the halyards the action of Budd's heart, intensified by extraordinary emotion at its climax, abruptly stopt—much like a watch when in carelessly winding it up you strain at the finish, thus snapping the chain—even under that hypothesis, how account for the phenomenon that followed?"

"You admit, then, that the absence of spasmodic movement was phenomenal."

"It was phenomenal, Mr. Purser, in the sense that it was an appearance the cause of which is not immediately to be assigned."

"But tell me, my dear sir," pertinaciously continued the other, "was the man's death effected by the halter, or was it a species of euthanasia?"

"*Euthanasia*, Mr. Purser, is something like your *will power*. I doubt its authenticity as a scientific term—begging your pardon again. It is at once imaginative and metaphysical—in short, Greek.—But," abruptly changing his tone, "there is a case in the sick bay that I do not care to leave to my assistants. Beg your pardon, but excuse me." And rising from the mess he formally withdrew.

27

The silence at the moment of execution and for a moment or two continuing thereafter, a silence but emphasized by the regular wash of the sea against the hull or the flutter of a sail caused by the helmsman's eyes being tempted astray, this emphasized silence was gradually disturbed by a sound not easily to be verbally rendered. Whoever has heard the freshet-wave of a torrent suddenly swelled by pouring showers in tropical mountains, showers not shared by the plain; whoever has heard the first muffled murmur of its sloping advance through precipitous woods, may form some conception of the sound now heard. The seeming remoteness of its source was because of its murmurous indistinctness since it came from close by, even from the men massed on the ship's open deck. Being inarticulate, it was dubious in significance further than it seemed to indicate some capricious revulsion of thought or feeling such as mobs ashore are liable to, in the present instance possibly implying a sullen revocation on the men's part of their involuntary echoing of Billy's benediction. But ere the murmur had time to wax into clamour it was met by a strategic command, the more telling that it came with abrupt unexpectedness: "Pipe down the starboard watch, Boatswain, and see that they go."

Shrill as the shriek of the sea hawk the whistles of the boatswain and his mates pierced that ominous low sound, dissipating it; and yielding to the mechanism of discipline, the throng was thinned by one-half. For the remainder, most of them were set to temporary employments connected with trimming the yards and so forth, business readily to be got up to serve occasion by any officer-of-the-deck.

Now each proceeding that follows a mortal sentence pronounced at sea by a drumhead court is characterised by promptitude not perceptibly merging into hurry, though bordering that. The hammock, the one which had been Billy's bed when alive, having already been ballasted with shot and otherwise prepared to serve for his canvas coffin, the last offices of the sea undertakers, the sailmaker's mates, were now speedily completed. When everything was in readiness a second call for all hands made necessary by the strategic movement before mentioned was sounded and now to witness burial.

The details of this closing formality it needs not to give. But when the tilted plank let slide its freight into the sea, a second strange human murmur was heard, blended now with another inarticulate sound proceeding from certain larger seafowl, whose attention having been attracted by the peculiar commotion in the water resulting from the heavy sloped dive of the shotted hammock into the sea, flew screaming to the spot. So near the hull did they come, that the stridor or bony creak of their gaunt double-jointed pinions was audible. As the ship under light airs passed on, leaving the burial spot astern, they still kept circling it low down with the moving shadow of their outstretched wings and the croaked requiem of their cries.

Upon sailors as superstitious as those of the age preceding ours, men-of-war's-men too who had just beheld the prodigy of repose in the form suspended in air and now foundering in the deeps; to such mariners the action of the seafowl, though dictated by mere animal greed for prey, was big with no prosaic significance. An uncertain movement began among them, in which some encroachment was made. It was tolerated but for a moment. For suddenly the drum beat to quarters, which familiar sound happening at least twice every day, had upon the present occasion a signal peremptoriness in it. True martial discipline long continued superinduces in average man a sort of impulse of docility whose operation at the official sound of command much resembles in its promptitude the effect of an instinct.

The drumbeat dissolved the multitude, distributing most of them along the batteries of the two covered gun decks. There, as wont, the guns' crews stood by their respective cannon erect and silent. In due course the first officer, sword under arm and standing in his place on the quarter deck, formally received the successive reports of the sworded lieutenants commanding the sections of batteries below; the last of which reports being made, the summed report he delivered with the customary salute to the commander. All this occupied time, which in the present case, was the object of beating to quarters at an hour prior to the customary one. That such variance from usage was authorized by an officer like Captain Vere, a martinet as some deemed him, was evidence of the necessity for unusual action implied in what he deemed to be temporarily the mood of his men. "With mankind," he would say, "forms, measured forms are everything; and that is the import couched in the story of Orpheus with his lyre spellbinding the wild denizens of the wood." And this he once applied to the disruption of forms going on across the Channel and the consequences thereof.

At this unwonted muster at quarters, all proceeded as at the regular hour. The band on the quarter deck played a sacred air. After which the chaplain went through the customary morning service. That done, the drum beat the retreat, and toned by music and religious rites subserving the discipline and purpose of war, the men in their wonted orderly manner, dispersed to the places allotted them when not at the guns.

And now it was full day. The fleece of low-hanging vapor had vanished, licked up by the sun that late had so glorified it. And the circumambient air in the clearness of its serenity was like smooth marble in the polished block not yet removed from the marble-dealer's yard.

28

The symmetry of form attainable in pure fiction can not so readily be achieved in a narration essentially having less to do with fable than with fact. Truth uncompromisingly told will always have its ragged edges; hence the conclusion of such a narration is apt to be less finished than an architectural finial.

How it fared with the Handsome Sailor during the year of the Great Mutiny has been faithfully given. But though properly the story ends with his life, something in way of sequel will not be amiss. Three brief chapters will suffice.

In the general rechristening under the Directory of the craft originally forming the navy of the French monarchy, the *St. Louis* line-of-battle ship was named the *Athée* (the *Atheist*). Such a name, like some other substituted ones in the Revolutionary fleet, while proclaiming the infidel audacity of the ruling power was yet, though not so intended to be, the aptest name, if one consider it, ever given to a warship; far more so indeed than the *Devastation*, the *Erebus* (the *Hell*) and similar names bestowed upon fighting ships.

On the return passage to the English fleet from the detached cruise during which occurred the events already recorded, the *Bellipotent* fell in with the *Athée*. An engagement ensued, during which Captain Vere, in the act of putting his ship alongside the enemy with a view of throwing his boarders across her bulwarks, was hit by a musket ball from a porthole of the enemy's main cabin. More than disabled he dropped to the deck and was carried below to the same cockpit where some of his men already lay. The senior lieutenant took command. Under him the enemy was finally captured and though much crippled was by rare good fortune successfully taken into Gibraltar, an English port not very distant from the scene of the fight. There, Captain Vere with the rest of the wounded was put ashore. He lingered for some days, but the end came. Unhappily he was cut off too early for the Nile and Trafalgar. The spirit that 'spite its philosophic austerity may yet have indulged in the most secret of all passions, ambition, never attained to the fulness of fame.

Not long before death, while lying under the influence of that magical drug which soothing the physical frame mysteriously operates on the subtler element in man, he was heard to murmur words inexplicable to his attendant: "Billy Budd, Billy Budd." That these were not the accents of remorse, would seem clear from what the attendant said to the *Bellipotent*'s senior officer of marines who, as the most reluctant to condemn of the members of the drumhead court, too well knew, though here he kept the knowledge to himself, who Billy Budd was.

29

Some few weeks after the execution, among other matters under the head of "News from the Mediterranean," there appeared in a naval chronicle of the time, an authorized weekly publication, an account of the affair. It was doubtless for the most part written in good faith, though the medium, partly rumor, through which the facts must have reached the writer, served to deflect and in part falsify them. The account was as follows:

> "On the tenth of the last month a deplorable occurrence took place on board H.M.S. *Bellipotent.* John Claggart, the ship's master-at-arms, discovering that some sort of plot was incipient among an inferior section of the ship's company, and that the ringleader was one William Budd; he, Claggart, in the act of arraigning the man before the captain was vindictively stabbed to the heart by the suddenly drawn sheath knife of Budd.
>
> "The deed and the implement employed, sufficiently suggest that though mustered into the service under an English name the assassin was no Englishman, but one of those aliens adopting English cognomens whom the present extraordinary necessities of the Service have caused to be admitted into it in considerable numbers.
>
> "The enormity of the crime and the extreme depravity of the criminal, appear the greater in view of the character of the victim, a middle-aged man respectable and discreet, belonging to that official grade, the petty officers, upon whom, as none know better than the commissioned gentlemen, the efficiency of His Majesty's Navy so largely depends. His function was a responsible one, at once onerous and thankless, and his fidelity in it the greater because of his strong patriotic impulse. In this instance as in so many

other instances in these days, the character of this unfortunate man signally refutes, if refutation were needed, that peevish saying attributed to the late Dr. Johnson, that patriotism is the last refuge of a scoundrel.

"The criminal paid the penalty of his crime. The promptitude of the punishment has proved salutary. Nothing amiss is now apprehended aboard H.M.S. *Bellipotent.*"

The above, appearing in a publication now long ago super-annuated and forgotten, is all that hitherto has stood in human record to attest what manner of men respectively were John Claggart and Billy Budd.

30

Everything is for a term remarkable in navies. Any tangible object associated with some striking incident of the service is converted into a monument. The spar from which the foretopman was suspended, was for some few years kept trace of by the bluejackets. Their knowledge followed it from ship to dock-yard and again from dockyard to ship, still pursuing it even when at last reduced to a mere dockyard boom. To them a chip of it was as a piece of the Cross. Ignorant though they were of the secret facts of the tragedy, and not thinking but that the penalty was somehow unavoidably inflicted from the naval point of view, for all that, they instinctively felt that Billy was a sort of man as incapable of mutiny as of wilfull murder. They recalled the fresh young image of the Handsome Sailor, that face never deformed by a sneer or subtler vile freak of the heart within. Their impression of him was doubtless deepened by the fact that he was gone, and in a measure mysteriously gone. At the time, on the gun decks of the *Bellipotent*, the general estimate of his nature and its unconscious simplicity eventually found rude utterance from another foretopman, one of his own watch, gifted, as some sailors are, with an artless poetic temperament. The tarry hands made some lines which after circulating among the shipboard crew for a while, finally got rudely printed at Portsmouth as a ballad. The title given to it was the sailor's.

BILLY IN THE DARBIES

Good of the chaplain to enter Lone Bay
And down on his marrow-bones here and pray
For the likes just o' me, Billy Budd.—But look:
Through the port comes the moonshine astray!
It tips the guard's cutlas and silvers this nook;
But 'twill die in the dawning of Billy's last day.
A jewel-block they'll make of me tomorrow,
Pendant pearl from the yardarm-end
Like the eardrop I gave to Bristol Molly—
O, 'tis me, not the sentence they'll suspend.
Ay, ay, all is up; and I must up too,
Early in the morning, aloft from alow.
On an empty stomach now never it would do.
They'll give me a nibble—bit o' biscuit ere I go.
Sure, a messmate will reach me the last parting cup;
But, turning heads away from the hoist and the belay,
Heaven knows who will have the running of me up!
No pipe to those halyards.—But aren't it all sham?
A blur's in my eyes; it is dreaming that I am.
A hatchet to my hawser? All adrift to go?
The drum roll to grog, and Billy never know?
But Donald he has promised to stand by the plank;
So I'll shake a friendly hand ere I sink.
But—no! It is dead then I'll be, come to think.
I remember Taff the Welshman when he sank.
And his cheek it was like the budding pink.
But me they'll lash me in hammock, drop me deep.
Fathoms down, fathoms down, how I'll dream fast asleep.
I feel it stealing now. Sentry, are you there?
Just ease this darbies at the wrist,
And roll me over fair!
I am sleepy, and the oozy weeds about me twist.

For Further Reading

One of my hopes for this volume is that it will inspire you to return to Melville and read his works in full. There's no better starting place than *Moby Dick*, a monumental work of American literature. Sadly, the way in which it is often taught turns off many students; even if you didn't care for the book when you first read it, it is well worth another read.

Typee, *Omoo*, and *Mardi* are early sea-faring Melville: the gay reader may want to try *Redburn* first. *Pierre* is considered by many to be lesser Melville; however, it certainly has a cult following. I'm particularly fond of the abridged version edited by Hershel Parker.

For more information about Melville's life, one can hardly do better than the short biography by Elizabeth Hardwick (issued in the Penguin *Short Lives* series). There is also an abunance of literary criticism related to Melville. Gay readers with a high tolerance for the esoteric may want to check out the chapter on *Billy Budd* in Eve Kosofsky Sedwick's *Epistemology of the Closet*; less esoteric but just as enlightening is James Creech's *Closet Writing/Gay Reading: The Case of Melville's Pierre*.

Robert Drake's study *The Gay Canon: Great Books Every Gay Man Should Read* has a very brief section on *Moby Dick;* but for a general study of gay literature turn instead to Gregory Woods' *A History of Gay Literature: The Male Tradition* which covers Melville (and many other writers) in greater depth, and is a thumping good read in and of itself.

I am grateful to all of the authors mentioned above for their work and for, in one way or another, helping direct my own thinking about Melville and gay literature.

And I would be remiss if I didn't plug my forthcoming volume *The Gay Henry James Reader*. Please watch the Gival Press website (*www.givalpress.com*) for information about the release date.

Ken Schellenberg

Barnyard Buddies I *by Pamela Brown; illustrations by Annie H. Hutchins*

1ˢᵗ edition, ISBN 1-928589-15-4, $16.00

Thirteen stories filled with a cast of creative creatures both engaging and educational. "These stories in this series are delightful. They are wise little fables, and I found them fabulous." — Robert Morgan, author of *This Rock* and *GapCreek*

Bones Washed With Wine: Flint Shards from Sussex and Bliss *by Jeff Mann*

1ˢᵗ edition, ISBN 1-928589-14-6, $15.00

A special collection of lyric intensity, including the 1999 Gival Press Poetry Award winning collection. Jeff Mann is "a poet to treasure both for the wealth of his language and the generosity of his spirit." — Edward Falco, author of *Acid*

Canciones para sola cuerda — Songs for a Single String *by Jesús Gardea*

English translation by Robert L. Giron 1ˢᵗ edition, ISBN 1-928589-09-X, $15.00

A moving collection of love poems, with echoes of Neruda à la Mexicana. "Jesús Gardea's poetry awakens a distant, almost forgotten primeval yearning that compels us to find that elusive woman whom we have met only in our dreams, but whose presence we sense will complete us." — Carlos Rubio Albet, author of *The Neophyte: A Dubious Beginning*

Dervish *by Gerard Wozek*

1ˢᵗ edition, ISBN 1-928589-11-1, $15.00

Winner of the 2000 Gival Press Poetry Award. This rich whirl of the dervish traverses a grand expanse from bars to crazy dreams to fruition of desire. "By Jove, these poems shimmer." — Gerry Gomez Pearlberg, author of *Mr. Bluebird*

Dreams and Other Ailments — Sueños y otros achaques *by Teresa Bevin*

1ˢᵗ edition, ISBN 1-928589-13-8, $21.00

Winner of the Bronze Award - 2001 ForeWord Magazine's Book of the Year Award for Translation. A wonderful array of short stories about the fantasy of life and tragedy but filled with humor and hope. "*Dreams and Other Ailments* will lift your spirits." — Dr. Lynne Greeley, Professor of Theatre, University of Vermont

The Gay Herman Melville Reader *by Ken Schellenberg*

1ˢᵗ edition, ISBN 1-928589-19-7, $16.00

A superb selection of Melville's work. "Here in one anthology are the selections from which a serious argument can be made by both readers and scholars that a subtext exists that can be seen as homoerotic." — David Garrett Izzo, author of *Christopher Isherwood: His Era, His Gang, and the Legacy of the Truly Strong Man*

Let Orpheus Take Your Hand *by George Klawitter*

1ˢᵗ edition, ISBN 1-928589-16-2, $15.00

Winner of the 2001 Gival Press Poetry Award. A thought provoking work that mixes the spiritual with stealthy desire, with Orpheus leading us out of the pit. "These poems present deliciously sly metaphors of the erotic life that keep one reading on, and chuckling with pleasure." — Edward Field, author of *Stand Up, Friend, With Me*

Metamorphosis of the Serpent God *by Robert L. Giron*

1ˢᵗ ed., ISBN 1-928589-07-3, $12.00

"Robert Giron's biographical poetry embraces the past and the present, ethnic and sexual identity, themes both mythical and personal." — The Midwest Book Review

The Nature Sonnets *by Jill Williams*

1ˢᵗ edition, ISBN 1-928589-10-3, $8.95

An innovative collection of sonnets that speaks to the cycle of nature and life, crafted with wit and clarity. "Refreshing and pleasing." — Miles David Moore, author of *The Bears of Paris*

Songs for the Spirit *by Robert L. Giron*

1ˢᵗ ed., ISBN 1-928589-08-1, $16.95

This humanist psalter reflects a vision of the new millennium, one that speaks to readers regardless of their religion. "This is an extraordinary book." — John Shelby Spong, author of *Why Christianity Must Change or Die: A Bishop Speaks to Believers in Exile*

Wrestling with Wood *by Robert L. Giron*

3ʳᵈ ed., ISBN 1-928589-05-7, $5.95

A chapbook of impressionist moods and feelings of a long-term relationship which ended in a tragic death. "Nuggets of truth and beauty sprout within our souls." — Teresa Bevin, author of *Havana Split*

For Book Orders Only, Call: 800.247.6553
Or Write : Gival Press, LLC / PO Box 3812 / Arlington, VA 22203
Or Visit: www.givalpress.com

www.ingramcontent.com/pod-product-compliance
Lightning Source LLC
Chambersburg PA
CBHW030518260626
47157CB00005B/1799